QUEEN NANNY

& THE WHITE WITCH OF ROSE HALL

A NOVEL

BOBBY SPEARS JR.

Kingston Imperial
4045 Sheridan Ave, #360
Miami Beach, FL 33140

For information address Kingston Imperial

Rights Department,
4045 Sheridan Ave,
Miami Beach, FL 33140

First Edition:
Book and Jacket Design: Kingston Imperial
Manufactured in the United States of America

Cataloging in Publication data is on file with the library of Congress

Title: Queen Nanny & The White Witch of Rosehall

ISBN 9781954220645 (Hard Cover)

ISBN 9781954220652 (Ebook)

AUTHOR NOTE

Dear readers,

Welcome to the world of "Queen Nanny and the White Witch of Rose Hall," the first book in an epic fantasy series that will transport you to the heart of Jamaica's rich and captivating history. This book has been a labor of love for me, and I am excited to share it with you. When I first heard the stories of Queen Nanny and the White Witch of Rose Hall from my mother, I was captivated by their power and resilience. I knew I had to weave these tales into a novel that captured their essence, while also bringing to life the rich cultural history of Jamaica.

As I delved deeper into the folklore surrounding these women, I discovered a world of darkness and magic that I knew had to be shared with readers. I wanted to create a world that would transport you to another place and time, where the supernatural and the human collide in a battle for survival. This book is a story of women who have defied the odds and risen to power in a world that sought to keep them down. It's a tribute to the strength and resilience of women everywhere, and a celebration of the power that we all hold within ourselves to overcome even the most daunting challenges.

So, dear reader, I invite you to step into the world of "Queen Nanny and the White Witch of Rose Hall." I hope that this book will captivate your imagination, stir your soul, and leave you spellbound.

Thank you for embarking on this journey with me.

Sincerely,

Bobby Spears Jr.

THE OLD WORLD:
A FORGOTTEN TIME,
A FORGOTTEN PLACE

—

PROLOGUE

The jungle is alive with sound and movement and panic.

People are running everywhere, some shouting in terror. But others are focused, driven by a desperate need to get as far away as fast as they can.

Some help loved ones, desperate not to leave anyone behind. Others concentrate on self-preservation. For all of them, nothing else matters. They are all running to get away, with no thought to where, or what, they are running to.

Behind them, the men from the ships race up the sand banks, their sticks spouting fire and thunder, and behind them, more come, men with whips and chains.

This wasn't the first time they'd come. They always landed under cover of night and brought with them agonies that went beyond the flesh. They had ripped so many of the villagers away from their families and disappeared with them across the water to this new world of theirs. Those who fought too desperately, they slaughtered, not wanting them to infect the others with their rebelliousness on the long voyage.

It was naked savagery.

And now the men were back, and all any of them could do was run and keep running, praying they could stay ahead of their pursuers because to fall was to be taken, and to be taken was worse than dying. It was the nature of the hunt that the weaker would stumble and fall, their legs betraying them. The air in their lungs wouldn't be enough. The hunters would settle for those, reducing the hunt to the survival of the fittest, the strongest, the fastest.

But not all who stumble and fall will be loaded on the ships, and they know that, too, because they've all been left behind before and they've seen what happens to those who are too frail. They are left in the dirt. A few brave ones try to fight when they can no longer run, but what chance do they have with their spears against bullets? It is all they can do to dig their heels in and die free. The weakest are overwhelmed, disarmed, and slapped into chains before they are led back to the beach, bruised and bloodied and loaded onto the slaver like cattle.

But even those who somehow outrun the slavers must stop eventually, no matter how desperately they want to keep on running. Every ounce of strength in their veins and bones is spent. There is nothing left.

As the sun begins to set, its light no longer able to penetrate the canopy of trees and vines growing unchecked, those who have come this far work together to fashion makeshift shelters, knowing that, if the worst comes, they will need to defend against more common predators, whether they come on two legs or four, or slither on their bellies. The shelters are crude, and the fire they risk is small, even though they are sure the slavers have ended the hunt for the night. It offers little comfort.

Sleep is restless, sorrows are deep, and tensions are high, but they must rest. It is that or die.

When daybreak comes, the slavers move deeper into the jungle, hacking their way through the undergrowth. They pause every now and then to listen to the secret sounds of the wilderness, hoping to hear people, before pushing on. There are signs: tracks where the undergrowth has been flattened, branches broken, and leaves trampled underfoot by people desperate to get away. In the hunt, escape and survival are more important than caution and care, and hiding tracks takes time, and time costs lives, so they run, leading the hunters all the way across the land to them. Even a blind child could follow this trail.

Deep into the hunt, hours from the coast, they stumble across a clearing. There are rudimentary shelters constructed from scavenged material. It isn't difficult to imagine terrified and exhausted people hiding there to pass the night. What is difficult is to imagine them finding sleep.

There are no survivors.

The hunters see the torn and broken bodies, the ripped flesh and dark earth where blood has pooled.

The naked savagery of the slaughter is gut-churning. One of the hunters can't control his stomach and heaves into the undergrowth.

With no one left to tell them what happened there, they are left to draw their own conclusions. An animal attack? The only thing that is for sure is that there is nothing there for them; no human cargo left to take back to the ship.

Only then do the men become aware of a sound gradually growing louder around them. What began as a soft hum has increased in intensity, deepening and growing more insistent, until the air is filled with wings and the bodies are smothered by a swarm of insects.

The hunters have no intention of burying the dead, so they leave them for nature to reclaim, pausing only long enough for one of them to remove a golden torc from the neck of one of the corpses, the metal stained red with dried blood. Together, they hurry away, happy to put distance between themselves and the carnage they found.

If they stayed a little longer, they may have realized that they were wrong. There is a survivor. A small girl, eyes wide, watches them just as she watched the slaughter.

It will be a long time before she tells anyone what she saw.

ONE

TWENTY YEARS LATER

They whipped Kwasi.

The cry escaped through gritted teeth.

They used the horsewhip as punishment— keeping the pain at arm's length should the victim lose all sense and lash out—and every bit as often as an encouragement, in the same way the lash might whip a beast of burden into movement. The worst of it, though, was always when they used the whip as entertainment.

The men and women, all dressed in their finery, enjoyed making him watch while they passed Afua among them. She was one of the young women who had come over on the same slaver that had carried him to this new world; a woman who, in another life, he would have made his wife, for she owned his heart. And they knew it. Their hungry eyes, eager for the violent delights of pain and anguish, had been as much on him as they had on her as they had pulled the clothes from her back. They delighted in his helplessness as they ran their hands over her cacao flesh, as they suckled at her neck and laved their tongues down the ladder of her spine while she tried desperately to preserve her modesty. He so wanted to look away, but two of the men grabbed a fistful of his hair and made him watch, laughing as they did so.

He couldn't help himself. He begged them to stop, but his pleas only served to feed their pleasure. All around him, they laughed.

One of them bit her, deep enough to draw blood. It ran in a trickle from her throat. It pulsed in rhythm with her life.

The breath caught in their throats, a hitch of desire and hunger, of need and craving. They had to have her. To taste her.

And that was the final straw for Kwasi. He fought to free himself, lashing out at the arms holding him. He writhed and wriggled, twisting, his muscles blazing, but all the strength in him was nothing compared with theirs as they turned their attention on him. They tore his shirt from his back, taking turns with the whip.

Afua screamed, not for herself but for Kwasi, and took a backhanded slap across the face, the sound of it louder than the mocking laughter.

They drove him down to his knees and yanked his head back. He felt the press of a knife at his throat and begged them to do it, to slice the blade across his skin and open the last smile he would ever know in his throat, but they weren't about to spoil their own fun quite so soon.

They made him watch as they did things to her, unspeakable things. She was passed around from one reveler to another, to another, tasted, tormented, tortured, until they dropped her to the floor, her eyes unseeing, body lifeless.

Kwasi railed against the men restraining him. He could not hold back the tears.

One of the women, her skin so white it had surely never seen the sun, laughed the loudest. The other guests deferred to her, ensuring her pleasure and her humors were sated. Kwasi had not seen her before tonight. He saw few faces. Most wore masks to hide their true nature from the world, but he caught glimpses of them, unexpected angles, and would never forget their eyes. They kept the rest of the slaves out of sight. This porcelain doll drew her pleasure from the agonies being inflicted on both him and Afua, but like all parasites, her hungers could never be satisfied, not when there was an entire banquet of suffering hidden below stairs.

Afua's body lay on the rug of lamb's skin in the middle of the room. They ignored her now.

The only one who didn't was Kwasi. Looking at her was better than looking into the eyes of the revelers who were drunk on his pain.

Someone offered the woman the whip, but she shook her head. Instead, she turned her attention back to Afua.

The porcelain doll's lips moved, but Kwasi couldn't hear what she was saying. It was peculiar. The more he stared, the more obvious it became that she wasn't saying anything, but she commanded the attention of everyone in the chamber as if she was subvocalising a hypnotic charm. She waved her hand over the body on the floor.

Kwasi had seen something like this long ago, in a country far away. He had never heard tell of a white woman with the gift, capable of doing anything like this. He had no idea of what she was trying to do or even if she had the gift to use magic on the young woman.

Afua twitched.

It was barely noticeable, but Kwasi's heart soared at the sign of life. She wasn't gone.

There was, in that moment, the glimmer, the

whisper, the sliver of hope.

And that was always and forever the worst.

The white woman's lips twitched faster now, as if she had found the spark of life inside his love and refused to let it go out. Faster still, commanding her to live, for the strength in her to blossom and life to return where surely it had fled.

Slowly, Afua rose to her feet.

There was something peculiar about her movements. Unnatural. It was as if she had forgotten how to use her limbs.

She did not take her eyes off the porcelain doll of a woman, who motioned with her hand, only for Afua's own hand to mimic the movement. She reached up to the wound in her throat and rubbed at it, massaging the flesh to encourage the flow of blood.

Then slowly, rhythm seemed to take hold of her body, causing her to sway, then rock, almost like she was dancing, as she smeared the blood

over the pert rise of her breasts, the rhythm of
the dance taking hold. She moved closer to each
man in the room, performing for them and being
rewarded with cheers as more blood spilled down
the cage of bones that was her chest.

They lapped it up like it was the height of
entertainment. A hungry man leaned forward
and pressed his mouth to the flow, lapping it up,
much to the joy of the onlookers.

Finally, she stopped in front of Kwasi and
offered up her throat for his pleasure. He tried to
look away, but his captors held his head, forcing
him to face her.

All he could do was close his eyes. He refused
to look at the abomination that was his love.

He didn't understand what was happening.
Witchcraft? Did the white woman have that
power? Was Afua under her spell?

The gathering roared. The woman with the
moonlight complexion gave a smile, appreciating
the approval her gifts had earned. But Kwasi

knew with grim certainty that she could do much more. He had heard whispers of a legend, a threat used by the overseers, of a white witch skilled in the same dark magics of the practitioners back in the place he had once called home. She was no legend, this white witch. She was very much flesh and blood.

And if that was the truth, then death was better than any alternative she might conjure.

The grip on Kwasi's head released, and he slumped, his chin resting on his chest. He couldn't take much more of this.

He opened his eyes to see someone leading Afua out of the room. Her ordeal was only beginning.

Unsupported, he could no longer stand. The two men restraining him each grabbed one of his ankles and dragged him out of the room, his head hitting the concrete stairs as they hauled him down the short flight of steps, each stair hard-edged and painful. They dumped him, forgotten after a single, painful kick to the base of the spine and a contemptuous order: "Run along unless you want to join your girl in the unlife..."

He didn't know what they meant or if he'd even heard them properly.

It took him long enough to realize he was lying on cold stone and not in hell. He lay there in a world of hurt. His body was a mess of lashes. There was no position he could curl into that didn't hurt.

He needed to move.

He heard a sound he didn't recognize—a strange mewling and scratching, like something or someone trapped behind a door. The sound came from somewhere nearby, as well as a strong animal smell that stank of danger.

A single source of light burned somewhere above him, a thin sliver that crept beneath the edge of the doorway at the top of the stone steps. The door had been left ajar. He struggled to his feet, every movement triggering a dozen fresh hurts. The sound of his movement sent the animals—whatever they were—into a wild frenzy in the darkness.

He had never been inside the big house before, but now he understood why some of his fellow slaves had sighed their relief when he'd been chosen in the slave house. They had feared this place for good reason.

At the top of the steps, he paused to listen. It wasn't easy to hear anything above the sounds of the animals, agitated now to the point of frenzy. But, straining, he could make out muffled shrieks of laughter from somewhere farther along the corridor.

The corridor was lit by several oil lamps, along with moonlight spilling in through a pair of windows overlooking the lawn. In that darkness, he couldn't work out which side of the house he was in, but that didn't matter. He was inside and needed to be outside. Once he was, then he would have to run as if his life depended on it. Because it did.

He was about to run to one of the windows

when he heard a door open. Two people, talking, emerged.

One, he recognized as his master, the man who owned this house. The other was the woman who had forced Afua to do those things to herself. The White Witch. Just the sound of her voice was enough to ignite the fire of hate within him. There was nothing he could do. To challenge them in their own home was to die.

"Things will be changing very soon," she assured the master. "It won't be long before you are free to walk in the daylight."

"That would be a most welcome development," the man said. "I grow weary of this life of darkness and envy you your freedom."

"There is always a price to pay for change," she said.

"Is there? I do not see you paying anything."

"Because I have not changed, dear one," she said. "I have merely learned to do things differently. That is my gift and my curse. I have unlocked things I never thought possible."

They were getting closer, walking along the corridor toward him. Kwasi stepped deeper into the shadows of a doorway, silently dreading them coming for him.

They paused, inches away.

He waited.

The door closed, followed by the sound of a key being turned in the lock.

Sensing his presence, the animals in there with him grew louder.

He felt something brush up against his foot but could not scream.

TWO

He waited for what felt like hours rather than risk opening the door. His heart was in his mouth. Unable to hear anything through the thick wood, he kept imagining opening the door only to find them standing there, waiting. He knew that he could not stay there, though. The men who had left him in there would return eventually. And when they did...

Panic gripped him when he couldn't find a way to open it, no matter how hard he pushed or pulled at the door. He felt his pulse quicken, and his mouth was sandpaper dry. But then it gave an inch, not in or out, but up. It took a moment for his brain to register the movement and what it meant, but when he did, Kwasi stopped pushing and pulling. He slid the bulk of the door upward into the frame and tumbled out.

He'd been grateful his captors had removed

their manacles before taking him and Afua
into the room to serve as entertainment for
the assembled rich and powerful, but that was
nothing beside the intense relief he felt about not
wearing them now. Chained, he was a dead man.
Unchained, he had a chance. Not a great one, but
a chance, and he was determined to grab it with
both hands.

He was halfway across the immaculate lawn
before guilt wormed its way to the forefront of
his mind: he should have helped Afua.

That guilt nagged at him. He shouldn't be
running, not if it meant leaving her to them and
whatever fate they intended.

But it had already happened, hadn't it? The
worst of it. He didn't want to believe it but knew
it was the truth, so he ran and ran, without a
single backward glance.

In the distance, way off to the right, he could
just make out the dark shapes of the outbuildings
where his fellow slaves made their homes. There

was no safety to be found there. Not now. Though it wasn't as if there had been any. As much as he wanted to just slip back inside one of those doors and act as if tonight had never happened, he knew that he couldn't. Those so-called masters knew what he had witnessed. Not that he felt like he had the power to bring any sort of justice down on their heads. He had the voice of a mute in this new world, barely able to make a mewling sound no matter how fiercely he decried the inhumanity of the barbs of wire, the deep cuts of the lash, or the chains that bound them to whipping posts. It didn't matter that he had been here weeks or months, there was no getting used to the inhumanity of it.

To his left, a wooded hillside rose. It was a place the men whispered about during the long dark of the night, a place where so many dreamed of escaping. The woodland had become a place of legend among them, a haven were countless runaway slaves had made a home for themselves, free of the yoke of the plantations and their masters.

There was rumor of rebellion, of slaves being organized by a woman. Surely, they were only stories, though? But in every story lay a grain of truth. And if only a few were true, then wasn't that enough?

In that moment, the truth didn't matter to Kwasi; he had nowhere else to go. It didn't matter if he found them. Even dying alone in the jungles of home was preferable to what was behind him.

Kwasi kept on running, arms and legs pumping furiously, head back and lolling from side to side on his neck the more desperately his muscles burned, fighting for every new stride, and didn't slow down until he was no more than a few long steps from the tree line.

Hands on his knees, gasping for breath, the salt of his sweat making the cuts on his body cry out in a symphony of pain, he turned to finally look back, but only because safety was so close.

Five steps and he'd disappear into the trees. All he had to do was keep moving forward, and his master would never find him.

But that wasn't why he looked back.

She was. Afua.

He made a silent promise to her, to himself, witnessed by the universe, that he would come back for her and set her free.

The windows were still filled with flickering light. They were still reveling in whatever depravities that fired their souls. With luck, that meant no one had noticed his absence. After all, what was he but a toy to them? He'd been cast aside as they had moved on to something else for their enjoyment.

He heard a howl coming from somewhere in the vicinity of the huge plantation house. It was a bestial, animalistic sound, and it filled him with panic.

As the guttural howls intensified, the sick feeling in his gut solidified. Had they released the dogs to run him down? Or worse, had whatever that thing was that he'd heard in that cellar been turned loose to hunt?

Kwasi began to run again, blindly this time, stumbling into the darkness of the trees and not stopping for anyone—or thing.

Several times, he fell, his feet tripping over roots, deadfalls, and other unseen entanglements in the undergrowth as he sprawled to the dirt. But each time, he got up again and forced himself to run on, finding reserves of energy he had never known himself capable of. But then, he had only ever run for his freedom. Now he was running for his life.

With every fall, the sounds of pursuit grew louder.

Closer.

He stumbled again, only this time, he felt a searing pain in his leg. He clamped a hand over the source of the pain. It came away wet.

Kwasi tried to stand, but the leg could barely

take his weight. He attempted to keep moving, limping and lurching from one tree to the next, needing them for support. Once they picked up the scent of blood, the beasts would run him down in seconds. He was already dead, only his heart didn't know it, even if his head did.

He saw a shape among the dark trees and heard the crash and rush of noise as something charged toward him through the undergrowth. Yellow eyes pierced the gloom. He saw the wicked gleam of teeth.

It leaped.

Kwasi knew without a shadow of a doubt that his race was over, and he had lost.

***

The beast stopped short of him.

So close he could reach out to it. So close its teeth could snap shut around his questing arm.

Neither happened. The creature let out a

hideous howl of agony and fell back, howling
again before scrambling away.

Two more pairs of yellow eyes appeared
behind it, a deep-throated growl sending a shiver
down the ridges of Kwasi's spine.

He scrambled back, heels kicking at the dirt,
hands slapping at a deadfall as if every inch
would somehow take him closer to safety.

The eyes did not come any closer. He heard
the slow, regular, deep breathing; the venting of
air; the rise and fall of barreled rib cages.

But there were other noises in the darkness,
too, these coming from behind him.

He didn't know which way to turn—not that
he could run, anyway.

Kwasi pressed his back up against a tree
trunk, whispering a silent prayer to a god he
didn't believe in.

The answer came in a low, whispered voice:
"Quickly! This way."

It was a man's voice. He felt himself being

dragged up to his feet despite the fact he had no strength left in his legs.

"Lean on me."

The man supported him, offering whispers of encouragement and urging him to dig deeper, to find the strength he knew he had in him, because it meant life and that was worth all the pain in the world to cling to.

Kwasi couldn't spare the breath to ask any questions. It didn't matter where they were going, who his savior was, or what was going to happen to him once they got there because whatever lay ahead had to be better than what he was leaving behind.

And somehow, he found the strength to keep putting one foot in front of another, stumbling on.

"Almost there," the man said when Kwasi stumbled again. The pain in his leg intensified every step of the way. It hurt too much to put any weight on it. Without the man, he would have fallen and not gotten back up again. He needed to rest, but stopping meant dying because those yellow eyes weren't going to be put off the tempting feast he represented. Thinking of the beasts and their wicked teeth, he realized he couldn't hear the heavy breathing anymore. He listened for the padded footfalls of a dog through the undergrowth—it wasn't a dog, though, was it? Dogs didn't have those jaundiced eyes—but heard nothing.

He had to keep going.

Every new step was a labored agony. But eventually, he heard voices, and through the trees ahead of him, he saw lights. The sight of them lit a fire in his heart and gave him the last burst of strength to push.

The man called out for help. People came running. In a moment, other arms helped support him, relieving his savior of the burden, and Kwasi managed to mumble an exhausted word of thanks that barely shaped into the actual syllables.

The relief was overwhelming. It was all he could do not to collapse into it. He felt himself being laid down on something soft, and then there was nothing but darkness that seemed to go on forever.

He heard voices in the dark, speaking in a hushed tone, urgent, but it was impossible to hold the substance of those sounds and turn them into words. And so he slept until morning, the deepest sleep he'd had for a long time.

***

Kwasi woke to the gentle touch of someone attending to the would on his leg. Despite their tenderness, the lancing pain was acute. He'd been dreaming of giant dogs tearing at his flesh, and that pain was their teeth sinking into him.

"I'm sorry," the woman soothed. "Foolishly, I had hoped I could take care of this without waking you..."

Breathing heavily as if he'd been running through his dreams, Kwasi assured her, "It's all good." And then the next thought, the next question. "But it isn't, is it? How bad is it?"

"It's not good," she agreed. "I've seen worse." She laughed. "But then, we had to cut the leg off to save his life... so, let that be your guide." A small smile played over her lips then, and she assured him, "You'll be fine if you let me tend to you. After that, rest easy. Time is the only thing that will heal you."

There was something in the way she spoke that made him trust her completely. It wasn't her voice or her manner, but rather the sense of calmness about the woman, the serenity, that instilled confidence in the wounded man. If she had told him that there was no choice but to remove his leg, he would have believed her and trusted her to do everything necessary to save him. She was a striking woman, with her hair woven into neat cornrows that cascaded into beaded braids down her back, and piercing eyes of ice the like of which he'd never seen before.

"Thank you," he said. "What should I call you? Mistress?"

She smiled. It was one of the first easy smiles he'd seen since he'd been taken from his homeland. "Nothing so grand, young man. Why don't you call me Nanny? Everyone else does."

"Nanny," he repeated. "I'm Kwasi, but they call me Thomas here."

"No, my friend, they call you Thomas back there. Here, you are among your own. Here, you are Kwasi. No one has the right to give you a new name. That is the gift of your mother and father."

He nodded. "What is this place?"

He knew the answer but needed to hear her say it. Instead, all she said was, "It's a safe place. That is all you need to know. More answers can wait until you're feeling better."

He found himself nodding, but even as he did, he said, "There's something you need to know..."

He expected her to shush him, but she didn't. Instead, she settled down on the floor beside him.

"Is it about a girl?" she asked.

"I suppose."

"Is it about the way that the white folks treated you? The things they did to you?"

He nodded, tears in his eyes as found himself back there, remembering.

"Is it also about the things that chased you into the forest?"

He nodded. "You know about them?"

She smiled. "Who do you think stopped them, Kwasi? Yes, we know what is happening in the big houses. But, for now at least, you have no need to worry about any of it. You are safe here."

"But what about Afua? We have to get her out of there."

"The girl?"

He nodded, a smile creeping onto his lips. He couldn't help himself. Just thinking about her brought him a small flicker of joy, even if the fear was quick to chase it away.

"I can make no promises, but I will speak to the others. But you need to be prepared... she is almost certainly gone."

He didn't need to ask what she meant by that. It was enough that she was willing to think about saving her. It was more than he could reasonably have hoped for.

Without thinking, he reached out for the wound, the pain in his leg making it hard to think about doing anything stupid like trying to save the girl he loved.

THREE

Kwasi must have slept again, despite the pain.

He had vague memories of waking intermittently and catching glimpses of shadows moving about and snatches of conversation, muted so low the voices didn't carry. Unsure of when he was awake and when he was dreaming, he focused on the pain because it was the only real thing in his life. The woman returned at least once to dress his wound while he was caught in a delirium that blurred what was real and what was not.

Night became day became night became day again and again before he woke, feeling more alive than he had any right to.

"So you are back with us, my friend?" The speaker was a man. He sat on the floor where the woman had been before. The voice sounded familiar. "How bad do you feel?"

"Terrible," he said.

"Good, good," the man said. "That means you are alive. Worry when it doesn't hurt anymore. Now come. Wash yourself and follow me."

"Was it you, last night?" Kwasi asked.

"Last night?"

"Yes. Was it you that saved me from whatever those things were?"

The man laughed, though not unkindly. "Ah, friend Kwasi, that wasn't last night. That was three nights ago. But yes, I helped you."

"How can I have slept that long?" He shook his head.

"The fever held you in its grip."

He thought about what the stranger had said, and rather than ask about the fever, he asked, "How do you know my name?"

A broader smile this time. "Everybody knows your name. You told us when you arrived. My name is Lima. But please, you must wash and dress now." He pointed toward a bowl of water and what Kwasi guessed were a shirt that had been white once and a pair of loose-fitting cotton trousers. "Do you need any help?"

"No," Kwasi said, "I'll manage." Though in truth, he had no idea if he would even be able to stand.

Gritting his teeth, he pushed himself up. He needn't have worried. His leg ached as he rose from the mat that had served as his bed, but the pain soon eased. The woman who had tended his wounds was as skilled as any of the healers back home. That was something he had never expected to encounter in this strange wilderness.

Kwasi allowed himself a moment to take in the shelter around him. The walls were woven reeds with mud daubed over them to bind them together. There was a smell to it that suggested dung as well as mud. Four paces across, there was little in it that suggested that it was anyone's permanent home; rather, it was a place to stay. There was a cot with a blanket and not much else. But he found himself wondering if it might become home if he remained. It had been a lifetime since he had felt as if he belonged anywhere, and even letting himself wonder was opening his heart to a world of hurts.

When he was ready, Kwasi pushed aside the curtain of vines that created a fly screen and stepped out into the open air. The sunshine beat down on him. He saw a surprising number of huts like the one he had sheltered in. It was a village, a community. He couldn't tell how many huts there were, though some, he noticed, seemed more permanent, and had more substantial wooden walls rather than reeds.

Lima was waiting for him. Kwasi asked, "What is this place?"

"Ah, my inquisitive friend, we are going to see the queen. She will answer all your questions, I am sure."

"Queen?"

"No more questions," he said.

"I just—"

"Not until she has decided if you can stay. Patience."

The possibility that he may not be allowed to stay hadn't even crossed his mind. He had thought he'd found a sanctuary. To be denied it was worse than having never found it at all. The thought that he might be forced to run again filled him with dread.

He felt Lima's hand on his arm. His grip wasn't tight, but it was firm, steering him toward where he needed to go. Kwasi didn't move to shake him off.

They passed among huts and after a few moments found themselves in an open space. There were thirty or forty women of all ages, from girls at their mother's knee to grandmothers with a lifetime of living written deep into their faces, gathered in a crowd. He was surprised by the lack of men. All heads turned his way, all eyes on him. Beyond them, sitting on the stump of a tree, he saw the woman who had tended to his wounds. She was younger than he remembered. A small fire burned in front of her. The press of women opened to let them through.

"Welcome, Kwasi. Please, sit," the young woman said.

The grip on Kwasi's arm tightened a little, making sure that he did as he was told. Kwasi and Lima lowered themselves to sit on the ground cross-legged.

"I don't understand," Kwasi said after he sat on the ground. "You're a queen? I thought... You healed me..."

"It is only a name. There is no royal blood in my veins. I am no more and no less than you or any one of these women here, though they decided I should be queen, and who am I to say no to such a grand name?" she said, offering a self-deprecating smile. He wasn't sure he believed her. "But that's not important."

"No?"

"No. What is important is what we're going to do with you."

"You can't send me back," he said before she could even suggest it. "If that's what you intend... just kill me and be done with it, please. Because I would rather be dead than go back there. You don't know what I've seen... I can't go back."

"I think I do," she assured him, her voice gentle. "I have seen things you could not even dream in the grips of the worst fever. Now I would like to know you story, Kwasi. Why are you here?"

And so, Kwasi told her what there was to tell, everything that had happened that night, down to the smallest detail.

Queen Nanny pushed and probed, gently teasing more from him. Her voice barely rose above a whisper.

But it worked. He described the horrors they had done to Afua, the things they had forced her do to herself. All of it. And it hurt him to remember, but he needed them to understand. He told Queen Nanny about how he had felt down there in the dark, hiding on those cold, stone steps while something prowled down there, growling.

He felt as if he had to answer her no matter what she asked, whatever secrets she dug for, even if they were not his to share. And in every instance, he answered as honestly as he knew how. He told her how he had fled, his eyes on the trees, thinking it meant safety, and swore on his life he would never tell the English where they were, even if they cast him out.

He couldn't have explained why he felt the need to make that promise, only that it seemed important that he did. He knew what would happen if he betrayed Queen Nanny and her people. That was enough.

When her questions finally dried up, his head was thick and heavy, his voice hoarse. The sun had passed its midday zenith. He had been talking for hours, even though it felt like a fraction of the time. The small fire had long since burned down to ash, leaving an odd fragrance behind. He looked at her, waiting with a mix of expectation and dread.

Finally, she told him, "There is a place for you if you want it."

"I do, more than anything. Yes."

Queen Nanny nodded. "You understand that I had to be sure?"

"No... not really. To be sure of what?"

Her smile was sad now, and he knew she was speaking from bitter experience. "That you had not been sent by the English to betray us. We will not be made fools of again. This place will remain a sanctuary for those who need it."

"Thank you."

"Our kindness isn't freely given, you understand. You know much about what is going on at the rich men's houses. It is my hope that you will help us fight back. Together, we are strong. Alone, we are weak. They want to keep us alone, to subjugate us."

"You have my help, any that I have to give," Kwasi promised.

The sound of hands pounding the ground signified the gathered women's approval. He turned to look at them, surprised to see that there were considerably more people to witness his joining of their tribe as had been there when he had taken his place in the center of the ring.

"Good. This pleases me, Kwasi. There will be much to do in the coming days, but for now, if there is anything you need, Lima will help you. Welcome home, my friend. Welcome to the Maroons."

He had heard the name, of course he had. Slaves who escaped their masters and formed settlements of their own, free places where their people could feel some sense of home and what had been lost, even if it was a daily struggle to survive the brutal attacks of the colonists and the hardships that came with living off the land. He'd heard one name, Mackandal, a houngan or voodoo priest, who had become a mythic figure among the slaves, with his rebellion against the plantation owners on another island. All of the islands had their own versions of Mackandal, but he'd thought they were nothing more than make-believe, larger than life heroes meant to give hope to the hopeless: a group of people living off the land, invisible fighters striking back against slavery. No one knew who they were, nor how many they numbered, and any talk had always been in whispers, shared by those with nothing left but hope. It seemed he had been wrong.

Queen Nanny rose from the simple tree trunk that was as much of a throne as she had and walked away, leaving Kwasi emotionally and physically drained as if the life had been sucked out of him.

He had given up everything, and there was nothing left.

No, that was a lie. Now there was this, a flicker of hope.

His body could no longer support him. Kwasi slumped forward, barely able to lift his head as he went down.

FOUR

Days passed.

Kwasi recovered from the ordeal of his flight from the house, but the nightmares lingered. He might so easily have lost his life in that great hall amid the revelers.

More than once, they sent someone to him with an elixir, vibrant crimson, like blood, that they promised would help with his healing. He drank it eagerly, desperate to recover his strength. The third time it touched his lips, he asked the woman who brought it to his bedside what this most potent of drinks was. "Imperial Sorrel," she said, not meeting his eye.

"Sorrel?"

"A restorative herb. Nanny believes that once the essence, extracted from the leaves, enters the blood stream, it is good for restoring the soul against what ails it in this place."

He didn't understand, but nodded, and took another swallow of the sweet-tasting drink.

It was only when he had fully recovered both his strength and his senses that he began to suspect just what had happened to him while he had sat in front of Queen Nanny, and if he was right, then he understood why everyone within the Maroons was so in awe of her: this peculiar woman had practiced an art akin to the one the White Witch had used to control Afua.

The realization both scared and thrilled him. If anyone could save his Afua, it was her, surely?

There was plenty to do in the rudimentary village, and now that he was up and moving, he was given his share of tasks to help rebuild his strength by Queen Nanny and her right hand, Lima. There was wood to be cut and food to be found, though the area was plentiful in both, and there were weapons to be made—sharpened spears. Their diet consisted mainly of nuts, berries, plantains and other wild fruits.

Lookouts were posted to keep vigil—which explained where some of the men had been that first morning, if not all of them—watchful for spies sent into the woods by the English to find them. None appeared in those few days, but that didn't mean they could let their guard down.

Plans were being made, but Kwasi wasn't party to them. Lima answered his questions about most things, but not all. And not about that. Though the other man did promise the time would come. Soon.

At dusk each night, Queen Nanny left the encampment along with one of the other women. He was curious as to why she always seemed to have a companion on these sojourns. On the third night, he asked Lima where she went, and why she had her constant companion when she ventured out.

"Be grateful she does. Remember that night you came here?"

"How could I forget?" Kwasi admitted. "That creature—whatever it was—still haunts my dreams."

"Good," Lima said. "You should never forget. And believe me, there are things out there considerably more frightening than that. Vile things. Creatures of pure evil. That is where she goes each evening, and if she didn't, you would have died that night. The chances are we all would."

"How? She fought that thing alone?" Kwasi asked, stunned by the implication. "How?" He knew the answer but couldn't stop himself from asking the question.

"Because she can," Lima said. "Believe me when I tell you I have seen women who can work magic, but I have never met anyone as strong as she. Without Queen Nanny, we would not be here. It is as simple as that. Without her, we would be nothing. We owe our lives to that woman, each and every one of us here, and that includes you, my friend."

Kwasi nodded. He knew that it was true. He didn't waste the energy trying to convince himself it might have been otherwise; he would never have made it farther than that patch of dirt where Lima had found him. The only difference was it would have become his grave.

"So what were you doing in the forest that night?" Kwasi asked.

"Queen Nanny's magic may stop those things getting through to us, but it doesn't stop other natural predators—a fact I assume you are grateful for, or you wouldn't be here. So that's where men like us come in. We defend the encampment against anything human the plantation owners send against us. We have to be vigilant no matter what, because the alternative isn't death. It's a return to that half-life they chained us to before we found this place."

"How can I ever pay her back?"

"Such an honest question, it speaks volumes

to your soul, friend Kwasi. But trust me, you already are," Lima assured him. "You are playing your part in the running of this place."

"That's not enough. That's not fighting back..." And then the quiet part of his guilt found a voice. "That's not helping Afua."

"Afua? That's the girl you left behind?"

There was an edge to what Lima had said that sounded like an accusation in his ears, but he couldn't believe Lima meant it that way. It was all inside him, that self-loathing. It didn't matter to him that he had promised to go back for her; that voice inside would always hate him for leaving her in the first place. It didn't care that he had been helpless against their tormentors or that he had been so badly whipped he could barely stand. Guilt wasn't going to left him off that easily.

"Well, then, maybe we'll get the chance sooner rather than later, the Old Ones willing."

It was a spark, a light in the darkness. It was that hope, still burning.

"Tell me something, my friend. When you were telling Queen Nanny your story, you talked about these gatherings, parties of flesh that happened at the big houses, but you couldn't remember how often they took place?"

"I don't even remember being asked the question," he confessed.

Lima smiled. "That's the way of these things. She asks and you answer, even if you don't remember, but you only ever speak the truth. But your truth was less than we already knew."

"You know about these parties?" he asked, and then the horror of it sank in. "And you've done nothing?"

Lima wasn't angry at the challenge. It was as if he'd expected it. "What do you think we could have done? Honestly. Tell me. No, don't waste your breath. You've only seen one of them. They gather every Saturday night, their debaucheries going on deep into the early hours of Sunday."

All he could think in that moment was that

their revels went into the Sabbath, their drunken brutality spilling into God's Day. "They have their preacher read the Scripture to us..."

Lima nodded. "I'm sure they do. But they don't care about it. Their piety is all for show."

"I don't—"

"It doesn't matter. We don't need to know the why, only the fact that they are godless. But we need to know which of the houses will play host to the next gathering. That is the only way we help your friend."

"How many estates are there?" He had seen little of the island beyond the fields they labored in and the dock where they had made landfall all those months ago.

Lima shrugged. "Enough, but not all of them are host to this circle of pain. I won't go so far as to say there are good people among them, but there are more moral ones. They don't see the evil in what they do, only that they are different to us and that difference is God-given, so they decide they are closer to the divine. That is an argument for a different day. We think there may be as many as twelve who are, though, and that is too many."

"One is too many."

"That it is, that it is."

"So they won't go back to my master's house?"

"He is not your master and never was. But no, it is very doubtful the revels will return to the place you escaped from for quite some time. Months. And that is a lot of suffering and torment before it does. That leaves eleven others, but there is no pattern to which hosts on any given weekend that we can discern. And there aren't enough of us to rise against twelve houses. We barely have the numbers to mount an assault on one."

"So what do we do?"

"We gather intelligence. We learn. And that means dividing, watching from the shadows, and biding our time—even if we know that our people are suffering behind those walls. Anything else means our death, not theirs. We need to learn the pattern to their gatherings, if there is one there to be learned."

"It will take months..."

"And we have to be patient," Lima said, his expression giving nothing away.

"Patient? Afua doesn't have months... How many more people are going to suffer the things that she suffered?"

"Too many," Lima said. "No one should have to go through what you did. But I can't change that."

Kwasi had pushed his own suffering to the back of his mind. The damage that had been done to his skin had almost healed by the time he had woken properly from his fever-filled sleep. The scars were more mental than physical, somehow, and even those seemed unreal to him.

IN THE LAIR OF
THE WHITE WITCH
I

The woman they called the Mistress was not
one of them—not one of those strange creatures
cursed to live their half-life in this world, hidden
only to emerge come darkness.

She thought of them simply as the Others,
not like the poor wretches they kept in their huts
to work in the fields, men and women snatched
from another land; they were different. Others.
She never used the term to their faces, though,
as much out of deference for the people they had
been as out of any sort of fear of them. No doubt
the Maroons had their own names for them.
She'd heard some call them the enemy, which was
nothing but the cold, hard truth described in the
most basic of words. She was able to tell them
apart from normal folk in several ways, not least

the paleness of their skin, which was bleached of any pigment, and by their graveyard reek. They carried that stench of arrested decay with them, no matter how they tried to mask it.

These Others were children of the darkness, powerful beyond reason at night. But in the cold light of day, they were vulnerable, desperately weakened, and forced to find ways to defend themselves that included taming creatures of their own twisted breeding to stand guard and hunt down any who sought to harm them. However, the hunger for more remained an undeniable truth. They were not content with mastering the night; they wanted to own the day, too. That was why they had turned to her, accepting her entreaties. She would help them find a way to overcome this fear of sunlight.

Of course, it was much more than fear. She had seen one cast out into the full glare of the sun, only to writhe, screaming as their pallid skin blistered and smoked, within moments reduced to ash.

She had long suspected what it would take to allow them to walk in daylight and who might hold the key. The problem was always going to be catching her alive.

It was the woman the renegades and runaway slaves called their queen, Nanny. She had never seen her, even from afar, but she recognized the magic's taint on her. That marked her as the one. The true enemy here.

The Mistress knew how fiercely loyal those Maroons were, to the point of self-sacrifice. They would willingly die to protect their Queen Nanny. What they didn't know was that there was nothing in their armory that was anywhere near as potent as the magic she carried inside her.

The Mistress could taste the source of the woman's magic, even from here. She knew it because she had been touched by something similar herself in what felt like a lifetime ago, and its loss was something she had craved ever since, despite the fact it had never been more than a fleeting contact, a brush with the true power of the old ways. That moment had given her insight into the kind of unimaginable things that could well be possible with that kind of power harnessed.

She had the talent to mimic some of the other woman's skills, but they were a pale imitation of the real dark arts of the old world she had never called home.

Those gifts she possessed provided little more than entertainment for the Others and were not enough to keep her safe from their appetites forever. Just for a while. At least, it pleased them to have her turn slaves into puppets and make them dance during their parties. But that pleasure would eventually turn to boredom. She needed something more to assure her usefulness. Something that would surprise them. Something that would stir their hungers. Something they had never seen before in all their long years.

It had been too long since the last party. She hungered for that contact with the essence of life stolen again. The need was growing stronger and stronger within her, an addiction she couldn't break. But with their supply of bodies, she had no need to.

The naked woman lay on the floor, life ebbing away from her as the onlookers simply watched, some smiling coldly, finding her plight most enjoyable.

Human life was theirs for the taking and using as they saw fit. Humans were worth less than nothing. The only thing about them that had any intrinsic value to the Others was the blood that pumped through their weak bodies.

But for all their arrogance and strength, the Mistress was capable of torments they couldn't even imagine in the darkest of nights. While they could bend the living to their will, even to the point of shedding years and changing their appearance, there was nothing they could do to the dead or those close to it. The dead were immune to the dark desires of the Others, but not to the Mistress's gift.

She reached out, feeling the last flickering spark of life in the woman, though in truth, it was barely enough to be called that. She could have snuffed it out in an instant without a second thought. It was barely a short-burning match flame, but it was enough.

She curled a finger in the woman's direction and raised her hand, barely concealing her smile as the body on the floor twitched. Yes, it was enough.

She motioned with her other hand, her lips moving to form a subvocalised incantation released on a breath that no one could hear.

Slowly, with no control of her bones, the woman rose unsteadily to her feet.

Her head lolled on her neck, eyes glazed. Her left arm hung slackly, broken at the elbow. Her hip displaced, one leg seemed unnaturally longer than the other.

But she stood, despite all that pain. She stood.

The connection grew deeper between them. The Mistress nourished it. Rather than merely controlling the slave's body, she was inside it.

She initially felt all the woman's pain, flooding her mind in a glorious burst of agony. She was forced to set it aside to savor the feel of being inside a young body again. It was delicious. She had experienced this revitalization more than once during her unnaturally long life. But then, two hundred years was a lot of lost youth to be recaptured one stolen body at a time.

On feet that struggled to find balance, she had the woman approach one of the Others and forced her head up, smiling for it. She made her hands run over her small breasts, smearing slick blood that glistened in the candlelight all over her ebony skin.

Her puppet moved around her audience, dancing for them, looking into the eyes of the

Others, who watched her with hunger and arousal in their eyes.

She guided the woman's hands down her abdomen, lingering on the washboard ridges of her belly before coming to rest at the top of her thighs, fingers exploring as she sought gratification, but it was the Mistress who gave the gasp of pleasure and not the woman.

Laughter and applause rippled around the room, as well as goading, until the woman finally stopped, slumping into the lap of one of the Others, spent and released. One arm draped around his neck, and she offered her throat so he could satisfy himself in the manner he truly craved.

The Mistress sank back into her seat, satisfied both by her work and her own physical response, which was more rewarding than if it had been her own body responding to those pleasures.

For a moment, she considered maintaining the contact, staying with the woman as she was passed around the room, bled, groped, and inevitably taken to one of the bedrooms to satiate their true hunger.

There might well have been pleasure to be found behind that closed door, but it would drain her to the point of vulnerability, and there was no telling what the Others were capable of when their darkest desires were given free rein.

It could only ever be a matter of time before one of them decided she could be the object of their amusement. Lust, especially blood lust, was the hardest of emotions to resist. It didn't matter that her body was not as young and firm as the woman they fed on. Hers had a power deep within it that promised so much more than simple sexual release. She knew that. They knew that.

But she could not afford to surrender her flesh to them for fear of what they were capable of once they had it. Right now, in this moment, they needed her because of the promises she'd made. But that need would change once she fulfilled those promises and they had everything they wanted from her. Then she would be as disposable as any other meat puppet.

She needed to find a way to give them what they wanted while ensuring her own safety. And that thought brought her once again to the Queen of the Maroons.

She was the answer.

She always had been.

FIVE

They watched and waited.

With the coming of dusk each Saturday, they went out in small groups, making their way to distant plantations to watch, needing to understand. Most times, they found nothing, though word got back to them that the unholy gatherings had gone down on the far side of the island. There were more than a dozen of them on the island.

During that time, Kwasi and Lima grew closer, bonded by a rage burning inside them at the horrors of what was happening behind those closed doors. They took up positions along with a handful of others at each of the plantation houses, waiting for the carriages to arrive, or a single carriage to leave, meaning they were in the wrong place. Again. The futility of watching that one carriage leave was hard on them. Kwasi's instinct was to try and follow, but there was no way he could match the gallop of horses on foot.

This weekend, just as it had been for the last two, they lay in wait, their eyes on the plantation house where Kwasi had been tortured.

Their group was larger this time. Their numbers had grown with a handful of fresh runaways finding them, each bringing with them fresh tales of the horrors happening at the plantations they had escaped. He wasn't expecting to see anything. He'd given up hope, even though he would never have admitted it to anyone but himself.

But he was prepared this time. If he saw the carriage leaving, he intended to make his own rescue attempt. He couldn't leave Afua in there. He didn't want to think about how Queen Nanny would react to him going rogue, but he'd made his promise to Afua before he'd made his promise to Queen Nanny, and in his mind, that had to count for something.

They took up their positions along the edge of the tree line.

Kwasi was already imagining his route to the huts for when the opportunity to arose. He wouldn't fail her. He couldn't. He was all that she had.

Several of the windows of the plantation house were brightly lit. The house itself could have been the same on he'd fled, so similar did it look with its veranda and gables, the white walls and blind windows. The sun had long since set, and the stars were bright in the heavens.

He heard before he saw a carriage approaching. His heart stopped in his chest, desperate not to betray his presence.

He didn't dare move.

He didn't dare breathe.

Lamps burned on the outside of the coach as it thundered by, but it was impossible to identify who was riding inside.

None of them moved. He knew that it was

ridiculous to think breathing could somehow betray them, but he couldn't stop himself.

They looked at one another, then back to the carriage as it slowed to a stop in front of the house. A figure clambered out.

Kwasi heard a second carriage approaching.

He knew.

He knew.

But it couldn't be happening. They shouldn't be back here so soon. With at least a dozen other plantation houses across the island, it should have been weeks until they returned, even if most of them weren't home to the Enemy. Why here? Now? What did it mean?

"We should send a runner to the plantation, gather up the slaves... get them to join us."

"They won't. And even if they did, we couldn't do anything," Lima said. "Even if we had twice the number, armed, it is a fight we couldn't win."

"Couldn't we?"

"You've seen what they are capable of, my friend. Don't pretend you haven't. You know what their pets can do."

"But they could be... in there..." He didn't need to fill in the details or even say Afua's name. "I can't do nothing."

Lima looked at him through the lattice of shadows cast by the trees. "You're letting that girl of yours cloud your thinking, boy," he said. "Best you consider her lost because we can't fight these things and their pets, even if our numbers were swollen by hundreds."

It hurt to hear it, but Kwasi had been having the same dark thoughts for weeks. "So we just leave them where they are and let the masters come to claim more playthings?" The thought made him sick.

"The sad truth is, we couldn't cope with a significant increase in our numbers—not so many people, not so quickly—even if we freed them. And the risk they would pose to all of us is too great. We need to think about all the women and children back there in the camp. I know it's hard. I know it feels like we are turning our back on good people who need us, but this is a war. It isn't a single skirmish.."

Kwasi was about to say they could leave the others, but he had to find Afua, when a woman who had come with them spoke up.

"He isn't wrong, though. We shouldn't just sit here on our hands. Even if we don't try to free them, we should at least try to find out what we can," she said. It was a point well made. It was, after all, why they were there. "Queen Nanny will want to know anything we can tell her."

"And if we get caught, Tula?" Lima asked.

"We won't. We take no risks. All I'm talking about is getting a look through the windows, not going inside. We'll wait until we're sure that they're all inside and drunk on whatever it is they drink and smoke in there, then I'll go down and see what I can see. The rest of you wait here, and if I don't return, you make sure the queen is told that we tried."

"I'll come with you," Kwasi said.

A moment ago, he hadn't been sure of her name. Now he was prepared to risk his life with her. This new life of his was a strange one.

Lima voiced his objection, but realized soon enough there was no stopping them, so he conceded with a shrug.

"We have to do what we think is right," Kwasi said. "Whatever the risk. The more we learn about what's going on in there tonight, the better we can prepare for tomorrow."

"Then go with the Old Ones, my friend, but take no risks. You come straight back when you have something to report. It's better for us all to get away from here having learned nothing than it is for one of you to be taken. Because as noble as your intentions, if they make you talk, and everyone talks eventually, you will tell them everything about us, and that will get us all killed."

"I wouldn't talk," Kwasi protested. "I'd rather die."

"That wouldn't help. Queen Nanny made you talk, didn't she? What if one of them can get inside your head and make you tell them everything, no matter how much you fight them? What then? How would you feel if your last living act was to betray the rest of us?"

Kwasi didn't want to remember, but it was there inside him, a visceral reminder brought back as fresh as the moment she had drawn everything from him without effort. And he knew Lima was right. He'd seen the White Witch make a puppet out of Afua and force her to entertain the men with little more than a gesture. She could well be every bit as powerful as Queen Nanny, or even more so.

They waited for more than hour, during which carriage after carriage arrived, the revelers greeted by the master of the house with warm embraces for the women, and polite nods for the men with them.

The moon was high in the sky, making it easy to pick out a path that, if taken, would keep Kwasi and Tula out of sight of the big house. Only when they were sure no one was patrolling did the pair step out of the trees and make their slow descent to the house. They didn't run because fast movement would draw the eye.

The walked slowly, in silence, full of courage at the beginning.

But with each step closer to the house, that bravado begin to seep away.

SIX

Kwasi made Tula wait for a moment before he would risk crossing the open-lawned area that took them close to the house. He needed to think.

They had clung to the shadows whenever they could, but now there was no choice but to step out into the open and all the risk that entailed. That last bit of courage was on the verge of failing him, but he remembered Afua and his promise, and he knew he had no choice but to take that next step. Their path had ensured they weren't overlooked by any of the lit windows, but that didn't mean there weren't a dozen other dark ones someone could look out from.

A dog barked.

Kwasi's heart leaped into his throat, fearing it was one of the creatures that had chased him. But a second growl reassured him it was nothing more than one of the slave masters' beasts, used to keep their slaves in line. It would be chained in the yard of one of the outbuildings, not roaming free. Even though it smelled them on the wind, he had to trust no one would pay attention because of all the comings and goings in the main house. It was a risk he didn't like taking, but what choice did he have?

"We need to hurry," he whispered, motioning toward one of the windows. "You take that one," he said, pointing to a window a dozen strides away, "I'll see if I can get a look through this one."

She nodded.

Close to the building, they moved fast. Their feet crunched on gravel as they took the last few strides, the noise impossibly loud.

The dog's barking turned frenzied.

Kwasi pressed himself against the wall and, in the silence between heartbeats, heard an impatient voice telling the dog to shut up. The hound whimpered but obeyed, and the world around him fell silent once more.

No, not silent, he realized. Laughter bubbled up inside the house.

He inched along the wall, closer to the window, and risked peering through the glass.

Inside, he saw the one face he had been hoping to see: Afua.

She was naked again, carrying a tray of drinks from lecherous man to lecherous woman, not so much as flinching as they caressed her skin. There were too many revelers to count. The room itself was gaudy with the riches on display.

He wanted to cry out to her, but the most he dared do was will the woman to be strong and reinforce his promise to her. He would save her. He had to.

As if she felt his presence, Afua looked toward the window where he hid spying. A shiver chased through Kwasi's body. It was as if her eyes were dead.

He pulled away from the window, heart racing.

Suddenly a man grabbed Tula, a large hand clasped over her mouth. She struggled, lashing out as she tried to get free of the stranger's grip.

A door opened, and a second figure helped subdue her. The pair dragged Tula inside before Kwasi could react. They hadn't seen him, or he would have been taken—or worse. The door closed behind them.

He had done it again.

He had failed another woman. He'd let her be captured.

His failure damn near broke him.

Everything he wanted to believe about himself had been undone in a few seconds of inaction, and worse, in those few seconds that followed, all he wanted to do was run. It took everything he had not to flee.

Instead, Kwasi moved over to the window Tula had been looking through, wanting to see what she had seen in there.

It was the room where he had been beaten.

He felt sickness clench his gut. Fear.

The two men bundled Tula into the room. She went sprawling, and in an instant, three of the revelers in all their finery were on her, tearing at her clothes while she desperately tried to fight them off.

It was an impossible fight. She couldn't hope to win.

Their mouths were on her, biting and sucking at her. Her screams were loud enough to set the dog off again. One of the men raised his face from her skin, his mouth smeared with blood. A smile crossed his face.

It was a face Kwasi recognized; how could he not? It was the man he had called master. He did not know his name. A slave had asked it once, on his first day, and taking a lashing for his temerity. Kwasi had not repeated the same mistake.

He stared straight at Kwasi and opened his mouth, revealing blood-red teeth that seemed impossibly large for his mouth.

The room erupted with cheers and laughter. They were loving it, their hearts fired by his debauchery.

Kwasi couldn't move. He knew that the master could see him.

Yet he did nothing.

The bones in Kwasi's legs seemed to melt, his feet unable to move even though all he wanted to do was run, and his mind was screaming to do exactly that.

The man laughed at him, smiling around those bloody teeth, then looked away. The spell was broken in an instant.

Kwasi turned and sprinted into the shadows, arms and legs pumping furiously, head down, driving himself on because he had to reach the safety of the trees before the beasts were released. He had to tell Queen Nanny what had happened. She needed to know what was in there... and what it meant for them all.

But the door opened, and Tula stumbled out

before it was slammed closed behind her. He saw the smear of blood on her neck shining in the moonlight.

Kwasi ran to her, knowing they only had seconds before someone decided to release the beasts from the cellar, because then it wouldn't matter how far or how fast they fled, those things would run them down.

He pulled up what remained of her torn and tattered clothes, trying to afford her a modicum of decency, but she was in shock. Tula didn't say a word, and Kwasi felt no need to encourage her to waste her breath. The trees seemed impossibly far away, but their only hope of safety was inside them. So they ran, not caring about being seen or heard now. She stumbled along beside him, with Kwasi dragging her.

The revelers already knew he was there—or at least, his blood-thirsty master did—so they would know where they could run because there were only so many choices.

What mattered—the only thing that mattered—was speed.

Kwasi ran until his legs were ablaze, every muscle on fire, and he kept on running, barely pausing to help Tula as she stumbled and almost fell sprawling. His chest burned with each gulp of air he sucked in. He didn't stop when they reached Lima, yelling for the other man to run, and kept on pushing through the trees, being slapped by their branches as they snapped back. He didn't grasp the fact that Lima was alone.

In the distance, he heard the beasts. They wouldn't reach them before they found the line of safety.

It was only when they'd crossed the invisible line of Queen Nanny's protection that Kwasi collapsed, strength spent, his legs unable to hold him up even when as leaned against a tree. There was still a way to go to the settlement, but he lacked the breath in his lungs to run another step.

"Where is Tula?" Lima demanded, standing

over him with his hands on his hips. He was breathing faster, too, but it wasn't stopping him from talking.

Kwasi held up a hand to ask him to wait for a moment, looking about him. Then he heard it, a sound from within the undergrowth where Tula lay curled up and cowering.

"They took her," Kwasi explained, still struggling to control his breathing. "The master... He tore her clothes... He bit her. His mouth was covered with blood, and his teeth..."

Lima was clearly concerned about Tula being taken into the house but didn't seem surprised by what had happened to her in there. "We need to get back to Queen Nanny," he said.

"Where are the others?"

"I sent them to warn her you two had gone to the house."

"Why not wait?"

"Because there was no need for them to be here." Lima shrugged. "There was nothing they could do to help you if things went to hell, and if they sent the beasts after you, their being here put them in danger. Better they were gone, back behind the wardings."

It made sense. As if on cue, the noises of the beasts came closer, but they weren't charging through the undergrowth this time. They were prowling. Had they learned the hard way about the potency of Queen Nanny's magical barrier? Were they wary of the pain it brought down on them, even if they didn't understand why it hurt?

There were more of them. There had been two or three last time, but now there were at least six of them out there; a whole pack of beasts on the hunt for tender prey.

"We need to go," Lima said, voice low and urgent.

Kwasi didn't argue. But before they could, they heard someone approaching behind them.

Whoever it was back there trod softly, barely disturbing the undergrowth, but they heard them.

Despite the fact they were on a well-trodden path, there was a lot of debris to be avoided in the darkness.

There was no lamp to guide whomever it was, but even as Kwasi listened, fearful, it was obvious there were no missteps.

Instinctively, he knew that it had to be Queen Nanny.

"Stay there," she breathed, her voice close to his ear. "There are too many of them, and there is no guarantee that the wardings will hold if they keep testing them."

She didn't explain more. She moved past them, closer to the sound of the growling, panting, baying creatures.

As exhausted as he was, Kwasi couldn't help himself; he edged forward an inch, then two, trying to see what she was doing. The near absolute darkness hid everything from sight.

But as he stared into the blackness, a sudden bloom of intense, yellow light lit the forest for yards around. It revealed the creatures on the other side of the invisible barrier. It was the first time Kwasi saw them for what they were.

He'd sensed they were larger-than-normal dogs, but their sheer physicality and enormous size took him by surprise. They were huge, clawing at the barrier by rising on their hind legs before falling back, whimpering as it stung them, then coming back for more, determined to break through.

But even with the light, it was hard to grasp their true size, in no little part because of the thick, black fur that covered their bodies and how it stood on end, as if charged with a shocking current, which made them appear even bigger than they were.

Their jaws drooled and slavered, teeth bared and growling. They were bestial.

If he'd caught even half as clear a glimpse of the one who'd hunted him that night, Kwasi would never have returned to the house. He was fond of this life, despite the path it had taken this far, and death was no place he yearned to be before his time.

Queen Nanny dug her hand into the dirt, closed her eyes, and breathed in deep of the loam before she tossed a handful of earth into the air. Vague, lightning-bright echoes of movement hung in the air for a second where her hand had been.

It fizzed and crackled as it passed through the barrier, causing it to shimmer an eerie blue so bright it added to the illumination from the fire.

The nearest of the things yelped like a puppy with its paw being crushed and stumbled back, falling. It bought little respite. Another took its place, snarling and snapping.

Queen Nanny paid it no heed. Instead, she began intoning a strange incantation, the words soft at first, then slowly growing in intensity as the rhythm became a breathless rush.

Kwasi knew none of the words she used. It was some language lost to time. But the magic did nothing to stop the beasts from clawing frantically in the air as they tore at the barrier, desperate to get at Queen Nanny.

Kwasi's attention, though, was on the beast on the ground. Its black fur had taken on a faint glow of blue, and the more he stared at it, the more it seemed that it fizzed and crackled. It was the same bluish glow the enchanted earth had added to the barrier.

Queen Nanny's voice changed, growing louder and higher in pitch until it reached a keening ululation that was enough to drive a sane man out of his mind.

Kwasi clamped his hands over his ears against the pain it caused. Lima did the same.

The beasts backed away from the barrier, still snarling at Queen Nanny, but without the same threat. They left behind the fallen member of the pack. It was changing, Kwasi realized, without grasping what that meant. He took a step closer to it, emboldened.

Somehow, the beast had become smaller, but that wasn't what twisted his gut. It was the way it had begun to look more... human.

Harder to understand: the fur shriveled away from its body, exposing black skin covered with a sheen of sweat.

It tried to lift its head off the ground, but it was a struggle it couldn't hope to win.

The beast's head was changing, too, its snout truncating, making it look less like a wild animal and, as horrific as the thought was to Kwasi, more like a man.

The creature—whatever it was—cried out in pain, its back arching as the joints and bones in that ladder cracked.

It let out one final, agonized cry, more human than animal now, and it was painfully obvious that the thing on the ground was no longer a beast, but a man just like him.

In an instant, the other beasts were on it, dragging the body away from the barrier. They tore at the naked man's flesh, fighting one another for a share of it.

Kwasi couldn't watch.

How could Queen Nanny just stand there, doing nothing?

She had saved the man from whatever magic had bound him, only to sacrifice him to the remainder of the pack?

All it had achieved was there being one fewer of them. It was only a matter of time before they grew tired with picking the meat from his bones and return their attention to Queen Nanny.

"Why would they turn on their own like that?" Kwasi breathed.

"They have no choice," she said. "The magic that binds them drives their actions and appetites as much as it does their appearance."

He wanted to understand more, but it was so awful. He wanted to ask why she'd sacrificed the poor bastard they'd just watched torn limb from limb, but before he could, the others began to howl.

Queen Nanny turned back to face them, serene, her entire aura one of calm, as if all of this was expected.

But how could she have?

Kwasi watched in something akin to horror as they all began to change in the same way the first had, slowly turning back into the person they had been before the transformation.

They turned on one another as they did; jaws snapping at flesh, claws snatching, tearing. It was carnage.

"Can't you save them?" Kwasi pleaded.

"I wish I could do more, believe me, but this is the only way to save them from what they have become. The dark arts that control them are strong, stronger than I am. But even if I were stronger, none can survive the magic required to banish it. The only mercy for them is in a quick death. Theirs will be less brutal than the first. It was his poisoned flesh has brought about their downfall, but they are what they are. Even knowing it would be their undoing. They cannot stop themselves from gorging on it."

It wasn't long before the bodies gave their last twitch and fell silent and still.

All six of the dead were black men. Kwasi didn't want to look too closely for fear that he might recognize one of them as a slave he'd thought had escaped.

Queen Nanny stepped through the barrier and sprinkled something on each of the bodies. She stepped back, and in a moment, they were ablaze, filling the air with the smell of burning flesh.

"Where is Tula?" she asked as she turned away, apparently satisfied that her work was done—for now, at least.

Kwasi went to find her in the undergrowth. It only took a few moments for him to help her stand and lead the broken woman back toward the others, but Queen Nanny and Lima had already started to walk away, keen to be out of there.

"At least there are probably no more of those things," Kwasi said as he supported Tula.

"Oh, you are sweet, you foolish summer child," Queen Nanny said without looking back. "You still don't understand, do you? They can make as many of those beasts as they like. They will have replaced those we freed by this time tomorrow."

If that night had taught him anything, it was that he knew nothing at all.

THE OLD WORLD:
A FORGOTTEN TIME,
A FORGOTTEN PLACE
I

"Hey, Nanny," the elder woman called. "Hurry now, girl. These eggs aren't going to gather themselves up."

The young woman looked up from what she was doing, smiled a little guiltily, and rushed across the yard to gather the eggs into her basket without saying a word.

But then, she hadn't said a word since she had walked into the village almost a decade before. The only sounds that ever came from her mouth were those of contented humming as she went about her chores.

She had arrived in the village with nothing but the clothes on her back, and even those had been torn to rags. If she had a name, she never shared it with them.

The elder woman had taken her under her wing, and while life had not been easy, the child had always been treated well. In return, she had always shown her gratitude.

Now she was older and stronger, a young woman rather than a girl, while the woman who had cared for her was being cared for in turn.

"They are coming, Nanny," the elder woman said when Nanny returned to her, eggs cradled in the basket she had made from woven leaves a month ago. It wouldn't last much longer. Nanny tipped her head to one side, listening to the air as if she expected to hear the drumming of hooves or the padding of claws and paws.

"Don't worry, they aren't close. It will be a while yet, but they will be here soon enough, my child, and you must be ready. You must practice, as much as you can, day and night, night and day, until we are both too tired to do any more. And when we have rested a spell, we must practice again. And again. It is our only hope."

The young woman nodded.

"You know you will have to speak eventually, child. You cannot master the magics in silence. Words are as important as any other component. So I'm begging you, find your voice before you are taken from here."

She had shown the young woman countless times how to set wards at night to keep the evil at bay: it was an evil that had always been in the jungle and took those who did not protect themselves. Nanny was bright, that much was obvious, but without her voice, she might as well have been a feral kitten to be drowned in the river.

The young woman looked up at her again.

"They won't take me, child. I am too old, too frail. There's barely any life left in my bones. Believe me, I am no use for what they want. The sad truth is that we have the weapons to fight the old enemy, but not the new one, and we are forever our own worst enemy, capable of horrors beyond any monster." She let that wisdom sink in. "But there are always other monsters than walk among us... Tonight, you will have to set the defenses around the village. I will watch you, but I need you to set the wardings."

Nanny was uncertain. She had seen firsthand what the old enemy and their pets were capable of, even if their true nature was beyond her ken. She knew they were capable of great evil and had watched them tear others apart.

Indeed, the first time she had witnessed such horrors, she had very nearly given herself up to the white strangers in the hope that they would protect her. But it had very quickly became obvious what they had been running from.

She shook her head.

"You must, child. Even if we are forced to pack our few belongings again and run, they will catch up with us at some point. There is only so much land. Eventually, we will run out of it and, cornered, will have to stand and fight. So do we run, or do we make our stand here?"

"Stand and fight," the young woman said, her voice raspy and uncertain, the first words she had ever uttered, as far as the elder woman knew.

She wrapped her arms around Nanny in sheer joy, almost crushing the clutch of eggs in Nanny's basket of dried leaves. "And you will set the spells tonight?"

Nanny seemed hesitant, as if doubting her ability to perform what was undoubtedly a life-or-death task.

"I will watch over you, I promise. I will not abandon you to it," the elder woman assured her. "But you need to familiarize yourself with the rites."

Nanny nodded and smiled that gentle smile of hers once more, sealing the deal.

Later, as dusk began to close in, they made their way around the village, laying down one warding after another, creating a circle of defense that surrounded the huddle of homes. While they would not stop the white devils with their weapons, there were other creatures, more immediately dangerous ones out there, who wouldn't be able to cross the invisible boundary as long as the warding was set right.

And there would be traps, too, for the more mortal threat. It took time, but the effort was worthwhile if it saved even one life.

It took more than an hour to visit each of the allocated spots, and in that hour, Nanny spoke a lifetime's worth of words, her voice coming in a rush, stronger this time, more sure of itself. She had listened and learned by heart every incantation the elder woman had woven in her presence. The words were engraved on her soul. The elder woman nodded each time, giving her approval and correcting her only once, and even then, gently, explaining that the warding needed to be slightly different in one particular place because of the meagre stream that meandered through the trees.

Done, they then took the time in that place to lay a very different kind of trap—one rooted in the old magics—in the hopes that it might bring them reward. It was tiring work, taking far more out of them than the short walk around the perimeter ought to have.

The amount of concentration required alone was enough to leave both of them exhausted. But it was essential work, with the others reliant upon them. The settlement was small, with less than thirty inhabitants, young and old, many having gathered after escaping the invaders. The ragtag band of refugees were glad of the protection the elder woman and her silent ward gave them.

Nanny had only the vaguest of memories of the woman who had given her life, and in truth, it was that last sight of her that stayed with her, her mother dead and broken among a massacre of bodies. She had rushed at one of the creatures who had attacked their camp in the dark, screaming at Nanny to hide. Her courage had been, ultimately, her sacrifice.

But hide Nanny had. She hadn't witnessed the moment her mother had fallen and had been too afraid to emerge from hiding to check the dead even when it was finally safe to. She had hidden while the black shapes had moved on the far side of the small fire—set when it had been decided the men had long gone. The few glimpses she caught of them made her think of golden wolves, but they were bigger, more muscular, their fur black and grey.

The thing had killed for the sake of it, not like other predators that killed for food, that took only as much as they needed, whether that food was man or beast. This beast revelled in death.

Nanny had pressed herself into the hollow beneath a fallen tree, burying herself in the debris of the jungle floor. She had left nothing beyond a small patch of her face exposed, not daring to so much as breathe, and even then, she had lain shrouded in darkness that would have been impossible for anyone to see her through.

She hadn't dared move for the longest time, forced to listen to the heavy breathing and the grunts and animalistic snuffles of the creature as it prowled, and then there was nothing beyond a deep silence when it was all over.

She had seen death before and knew that this was it. Even the sounds of agony, of the last dying breaths, were gone.

She had been too afraid to break cover, too afraid to move for hours, barely daring to breathe in case the thing came back. All she could do to take the images out of her head was to think about home and the life where she had wanted for nothing, wondering how she would find her way back there.

She must have drifted off to sleep. When she had awoken, she had been afraid to open her eyes, even though she only heard the familiar jungle sounds she'd heard so many times, the background noise of birds and insects. She heard something she couldn't place. A curious noise. For as long as she kept her eyes closed, she could lie to herself and pretend it had all been a dream, that her mother and the others were already awake and making breakfast. Perhaps they were getting ready to move on in case the men returned.

But then she heard movement and voices. She opened her eyes, blinking against the light and the desperate urge to rub her eyes.

The men were back, and they were close.

For a moment, Nanny thought about slipping from her hiding place and running as fast as she could, anywhere. But before she could, her eyes filled with tears at the memory of last night and the truth that her mother was dead, as was everyone else she had ever known, and her very being was frozen with fear.

There was a burst of movement as birds took to the wing, startled by the approach of voices.

A moment later, the men burst into the clearing. They stopped dead in their tracks, their voices silenced.

And in that silence, Nanny knew what the other sound she could hear was: the sound of thousands of pairs of tiny wings buzzing around the bodies of those who had protected her.

She stifled a scream, panicked that the men would hear her, but they were oblivious to everything apart from the fallen bodies and the mass of insects smothering them.

Almost as one, the men turned and ran, charging through the jungle as if their lives depended on it. One paused long enough to take her mother's necklace but soon their noise was little more than a faint echo.

Something settled on her face, and she knew that she couldn't stay there any longer unless she wanted more to descend on her. There were too many in the mass of tiny bodies locked in the feeding frenzy.

With no idea where she could go beyond needing to get away from this place as quickly as she could, she ran.

She did not look back.

SEVEN

"Why did you bring her back here?"

In the light of early morning, Queen Nanny was in a rage at the sight of Tula. The woman had been sleeping in a hut. Her skin was burning up but was an ashen gray. The wound at her throat had dried, but her flesh was stained with dried blood.

"What were you thinking?"

Kwasi was shaken but replied, "That she was one of us and that we should take care of her."

Kwasi had no idea what he had done wrong. Queen Nanny had asked where she was, so surely, she hadn't intended to leave her out there?

He glanced around at the others who had gathered there, Tula's friends and family, but from their expressions, it was obvious they knew something he didn't. No one said a word.

Queen Nanny knelt beside Tula. For a

moment, it seemed her rage subsided, and she tended to Tula's wounds with all the care of a loved one. She dismissed the others but bade Kwasi and Lima stay.

He realized then what had gotten under Queen Nanny's skin: they hadn't mentioned Tula's injuries. He stared to apologize, but she silenced him.

"I'm sorry," she said. "This is not on you. It's on me. You weren't to know." She turned to Lima. "I assume you didn't see her injuries or know how they were inflicted if you did?"

The other man shook his head. "No."

"I still don't understand what I've done wrong," Kwasi said. "I thought I was helping her by bringing her to you, so that you could do for Tula what you did for me…"

"Of course you did," she said. "And as I said, that is on me. I should have taught you better, given you have no concept of what we are up against here. You were there. You saw. You deserved to know what those things were. I am sorry for that." She applied a yellow paste to the wound on Tula's throat. The damage as not as severe as he had expected it to be.

In his world hurt was a simple thing; blood was blood, a wound was a wound, you stopped the bleeding, you saved a life. Or it had been until a pack of baying, yellow-eyed wolves had shifted shape to die as men in the dirt at his feet. He'd done the only thing a good man could: when they'd been running he'd been forced to tear a ragged strip of cloth and pressed it against the wound to soak up as much blood as possible.

But now when Kwasi looked at it, instead of seeing the torn and ragged flesh he had imagined, there were simply a pair of needle pricks that looked raw, perhaps with the beginnings of infection, and a halo of dried blood.

"The damage doesn't look too bad," he said over Queen Nanny's shoulder.

"That is because the true damage is on the

inside," she said.

"Infection?"

"In a manner of speaking." She stood up, tiredness showing in her movements. "Remember last night when I said that this cabal of plantation owners could raise their pets at will? This is what I meant."

Kwasi nodded, but was confused. "I don't understand."

"Which is part of the problem. They do this to them." She touched the woman's neck, and Tula's eyes fluttered for a moment before settling. "Sometimes it produces something different, something more like themselves. Other times, their gets are bestial throwbacks, like the things you saw out there."

"Like themselves?"

"They are strange creatures, far older than they appear and different in ways even I do not fully understand. But they are not human, for all that they look like us. They are monsters."

His confusion grew. He heard the words, but understanding and belief were harder concepts.

"There was an old enemy, back in our homeland... I think they brought it here, and now they sow death in this new island world of ours. They had no idea what they had captured. Fools."

He listened as Queen Nanny told tales of how these things survived on the nourishment of blood drunk from the veins of a living person and how in some instances they were more than merely cattle for milking, and that something was given in exchange, something that changed them.

He listened in the same way as he'd listened to the old fireside tales as a child, slack-mouthed with wonder and not daring or wanting to believe a word of it.

It was impossible. A grim make-believe. But it explained so many things.

The problem was, even as he wrestled with the implications of what her story meant for Afua and Tula, it raised so many more questions he couldn't hope to answer. Namely, what was going to happen to them?

"Can you save her?" he asked, not sure which of them he was talking about.

Queen Nanny shrugged. "I don't know. Maybe. Probably not. But sooner rather than later, we will have a difficult decision to make. And that is on your shoulders, Kwasi. Your burden. I shall expect you to be man enough to do what needs to be done."

He said nothing, not understanding.

"If I can't prevent her... change... it may well be too late for all of us. Do you understand that? This is like a plague. I fear that whoever bit her, whoever infected her with their magic, will be able to see through her eyes, hear through her ears, and, perhaps most dangerous of all to us, listen to her thoughts. That means they will know about us, where we are, how many of us there are, our plans—everything. We will be unable to talk freely for fear she overhears and our words carry back to her masters."

She used the same word he had to describe the plantation owner but meant it in a very different way. She wasn't talking about the slave masters. She was talking about the cabal of those wicked few who had more control of them than those who had staked their ownership on them, buying and selling their lives. Because, for all their power, they couldn't reach inside your mind and manipulate you like a marionette or sift through your thoughts, looking to use them against you.

"We can at least dream of our freedom," Queen Nanny continued. "But those who succumb to this ancient enemy have no such freedom. Believe me, if we fail her, it will be kinder to free Tula from those invisible chains rather than allow them to choke the humanity out of her."

He wanted to beg, to plead. But he knew the woman was doing everything she could, although some things were beyond even one like her.

"The next few hours will tell us whether I have failed her. I will stay with her. Go now, Kwasi. Leave me to my work. And pray to whatever gods you believe in. Maybe that will make the difference."

Kwasi backed out of the cramped hut but did not move far from the doorway. He was close enough to hear Queen Nanny's whispered incantation.

More than once, he glanced inside, risking her wrath, but she didn't notice, or if she did, chose not to admonish him. In the dim interior, he saw Tula's skin glowed a deep red as if fire raged beneath it. He couldn't understand what was happening but was sure the fire must be real because he felt the heat emanating from her as the fever raged.

Eventually, Queen Nanny emerged from the shelter, stretching and working the muscles in her back after hours of being cramped over Tula in the same uncomfortable position.

Kwasi rushed toward her, desperate to know how she fared.

Queen Nanny pre-empted his questions, simply saying, "All we can do is wait. She's sleeping now. But I have come to a realization, and for that, I owe you thanks. We cannot wait until their next gathering to take the fight to them. That will be too late. For now, though, I need rest."

EIGHT

Tula was still asleep the following morning, the fever having broken. Her skin was cool to the touch, the fire burned out. It was a restless sleep.

Queen Nanny had insisted on someone staying with Tula all night and making sure they understood how important it was they warn her if anything changed. While there were many willing to take up the vigil, Kwasi and Lima shared the duty out of a mutual feeling of debt to Tula. Kwasi would have watched her all night, so deep was his sense of guilt and shame, but Lima had insisted they share the bedside vigil.

Kwasi managed to get a few hours' sleep after dawn, and by the time he emerged from his own shelter—hardly refreshed—the encampment was abuzz with activity. He sensed alarm.

"What's happening?" he called to the first person he saw.

She didn't stop. She hurried to be somewhere else.

He spotted Lima in a huddle with three other men and hurried to join them. Their body language was tense, anxious. Something was wrong, and he didn't need to ask what.

"They were out early this morning, checking the bird traps for game." Lima nodded toward the three others. "Instead, they found three men hanging from trees at the edge of the jungle."

Kwasi cursed beneath his breath. Every lynching was one too many. But it was hardly the first time slaves had been strung up for trying to escape, so why the sudden panic? Were the dead men too close to the encampment?

"Where?" Kwasi asked.

"To the north of the island," Lima explained. "But they aren't the only ones," he added, and that went some degree toward explaining the reaction within the camp. "We've had two more groups return with similar reports—black men hanging from trees just at the edge of the jungle."

Kwasi's mind raced to the only logical conclusion: it was a message. "You think they are connected." It wasn't a question.

"Plantation owners don't kill any of us without a reason. They pay good coin for a slave. They own them. Sure, some might take perverse pleasure in horsewhipping or causing pain, but without our labor, the cane doesn't get harvested. Make an example of one to keep the others in line, yes. But three? Never. And from the sounds of it, those poor wretches were beaten half to death before they had a rope tied around their necks and were forced to watch as the end was thrown over a branch and they were hauled up off their feet. It's a barbaric way to die.

"For it to happen the same way at different plantations on the same morning? That is no coincidence. And no warning—at least, not for the slaves there. It is a warning to us. They know that we are here, even if they don't know exactly where. Because of their dead beasts, they know we are protected by powerful magic. No, this message is plain enough. They want to be sure we understand there is a terrible price to be paid for daring to go back."

"They did this because of me?"

"You were not alone out there."

"Where is Queen Nanny now?"

"She has gone to check that the boundary is secure." Lima looked uneasy. "She has been gone longer than I would like, but she was insistent that she needed to see for herself what has been done."

"What about where we were last night? Has anyone been out that way?"

Lima shook his head. "No."

"Then I will go," Kwasi said.

"We were told to stay here until Queen Nanny returned."

"Then tell her where I've gone. There are people I know out there... good people..."

"All the more reason not to go. You don't want to live with that in your head for the rest of your life. Trust me on this."

The way he said it left Kwasi in no doubt that the other man had his fair share of demons living inside his head that woke up when he closed his eyes. But Kwasi was already heading away from him. He walked toward the path that would take him down the hillside to the enclave where Queen Nanny had turned that pack of beasts into broken men.

He knew there was nothing to be afraid of there, but that didn't stop his heart from hammering as he neared the clearing, because too much of what he had experienced since that night in the mansion defied reason.

It didn't mean that there weren't other dangers to be wary of. During daylight hours, they shared the trees with all manner of predators, not least the men who would haul him back to the plantation if they caught him, then strip, whip, and break him before they put him back to work.

Or worse.

The one thing about that kind of threat, he could see it coming and keep his distance. And if they saw him, then he had to hope that the slavers had too much to do to keep them from chasing shadows among the trees. Of course, there was always the risk of one of them being hot-headed and going after him in a rage.

He heard Lima calling after him but didn't break his stride. He had to see for himself what was going on and wasn't about to let anyone talk him out of it.

He wondered briefly if Lima would follow him regardless of Queen Nanny's instructions but didn't give it another thought once he was clear of the man-made enclave and striding through the undergrowth. If he hurried, he might be back before Queen Nanny, and then she need never know that he'd gone against her orders.

He knew it was a thin hope. Even so, the punishment was a price he was willing to pay because he needed to know if there were more victims among those he'd labored beside. Not that he could change anything or help them beyond cutting them down and giving them a little dignity in death.

But he still needed to know. For there was one fear that he fought to keep out of his mind.

He lost his footing more than once in his haste, stumbling against a tree root and tripping on a trailing vine. But the closer he got to the barrier, the more he felt the need to rush, driving himself on and only slowing at the sight of the charred remains of the changed men Queen Nanny had destroyed.

There was little left, mostly ash and a patch of blackened ground. It wouldn't take much to make it look as if nothing had happened there. That no horror had taken place. He tried not to stare at the ash, but it was hard to resist.

He was still standing there, staring at the ground, when he became aware of someone standing at his shoulder.

"We should hurry," Lima said. "Whether we're going on or heading back, it is the same. We should hurry."

Kwasi nodded and picked up his pace again, breathing hard as he ran. The trees thinned as they reached the edge of the trees and more land set aside for sugar cane.

Out of the corner of his eye, he saw something moving. It was a gentle swaying, a shadow moving from side to side. If it hadn't been against the thick boles of the tree trunks, he might not have picked up the movement. It confused him at first, his mind unable to recognize it for what it was. But a few more paces made it all too real for him. He saw a pair of bare feet and brown legs floating above the ground.

The fear returned, urging him not to look, but he knew that he was going to. He'd always known that from the first moment his feet had put him on this path.

They belonged to a woman who hung from the last tree. Her body moved in the sea breeze that cut across the land.

He could still walk away if he wanted to. Last chance.

But he had to walk around her lifeless body. He needed to see her face, even though he knew who it was.

Afua.

He tried to convince himself that it wasn't her. Her face was a shade of blue. Her tongue lolled out. Her jaw was slack. But for all he desperately wanted it to be someone else, someone else's grief and pain, it was her, and it was his.

"We have to cut her down," Kwasi said.

"No, we don't," Lima contradicted him. "That's the last thing we should do. If they see we've cut her down, they learn a little more about us. They know that we care about one another, about those we left behind when we escaped. And that puts those slaves at risk. These creatures will use our humanity against us. They will kill more of their workers, and they will hang them up to taunt us, all around the jungle. Will you cut them all down?"

But Kwasi wasn't sure he was right, "They won't kill everyone. We have value. We do their work. Without us, the cane will rot in the fields."

This time, Lima laughed. "They don't give a fuck about sugar cane, and the only value we have to them is blood. These monsters aren't the same as other plantation owners. You need to stop thinking of them as normal people. They aren't."

"Why kill her? She served them... They got to use her body..."

"Because they know everything, my friend. They are party to every single thought inside her head. They knew what she saw. You said that you had seen her at the house through the window.

They would have known that she mattered to you. You got her killed, my friend. You might as well have put the rope around her throat. I don't say that to be unkind. But it doesn't matter. Check her neck. You will see their mark on her, just as it is with Tula. The plantation owners and their gang masters might own our bodies, but these fiends take our souls."

Kwasi didn't want to believe because believing made monsters out of them, and monsters were harder to kill than men.

Afua was dead, and there was no one left that he needed to rescue.

Now it was about avenging her.

NINE

They reached the village moments after Queen Nanny.

There was a quietness about the encampment that was unnatural. Normally, it was a hubbub of activity, with people knowing their duties and eager to get them done, but not today. Kwasi and Lima had gathered firewood along the way, returning with their arms full. Nothing was said about their absence.

Queen Nanny sat on the same tree stump she had when Kwasi had been brought before her. He'd come to think of it as her throne. Most of the inhabitants of the village had already taken up seats on the ground in front of her.

She motioned for them to join her. "Are we waiting on anyone else to return?" she asked, no judgment in her tone.

People looked around the gathering. There

were lots of head shakes. She began.

"I have traveled the island this morning and seen more than a dozen people hanging from trees. All of them, to a soul, bore the mark of the enemy, and as much as it grieves me to say it, none of them had an easy death. I tried, but each of them was far beyond my help."

Distressed sounds rippled through the onlookers.

"This was a message to us; I am sure of it. They will stop at nothing to seek vengeance. I am thankful it is daylight and we need only concern ourselves with their human servants, those without powers beyond the pistol, the bullwhip, and the rope. They are dangerous, make no mistake, but at least we know what we are dealing with."

She fell silent, lost in thought, her head lowered as if the ground between her feet had become the most fascinating thing in the world to her. When her head came up, there was a dark shine in her eyes.

"Night is a different matter. Under cover of those dark skies, the enemy is at liberty to hunt, and we have no power against them. Pity us all if they ever learn to walk in daylight . . ."

Again, she fell silent.

Kwasi felt the itch of a forgotten memory. He had heard those words before somewhere. Someone talking about walking in daylight. Where? When?

Queen Nanny stared straight at him. He nodded, though the response was automatic.

She continued. "We are fortunate that one of our number overheard a conversation in the home of the enemy. We know they are close to being capable of just that."

She was talking about him.

Even though he had as good as forgotten it, she had somehow managed to retrieve those words from his memory with her whispered questions. He had told her everything he had heard, even things he couldn't have hoped to understand the importance of.

"We cannot wait until their next gathering. We need to take the fight to them. But our window of opportunity is narrow and closing fast. We cannot hope to beat them at night, and in daylight, they surround themselves with their henchmen, servants, and guards. We have one chance to strike. Their weakness, such as it is, comes with the dawn, when they take to their nests to sleep the day away. We must find their nests and burn them out."

There was silence. Kwasi broke it.

"What about the beasts? Do they keep their human-dogs close to them?" he asked.

"They may well do," Queen Nanny replied. "I do not know the answer to your question."

"If they do, I know where they sleep, or at least where they rest in the plantation I escaped from."

He told the story of that night again, this

time focusing on something he hadn't known he'd learned hiding on the staircase. He had heard what he now knew were the beasts who'd pursued him into the jungle twice. They would be away from any danger of sunlight down there.

Queen Nanny nodded. Looking at her, he was sure she already knew about that place. Perhaps he had already told her about it along with everything else?

"We need to capture one of their pets," she reasoned. "But rather than turn it, we'll need to keep it alive long enough to learn everything it knows, which is dangerous to us. But they have seen things we haven't. If anyone will know what leads our enemy to believe they will finally walk in daylight, their pets will."

"Then we should have kept one of them alive last night," someone muttered.

"That was last night. Before their messages. It is easy to look back and think would have, could have, should have. We were not to know.

Besides, there were too many of them. I could not have isolated one without risking our safety. All it would have taken was one of them to breach our defenses, and everything here would have been lost. No, last night had to be last night, and tonight must be tonight. If we are fortunate, we may not end up as a feast for crows."

A whisper grew among the gathering and, with it, a sense of fear. Kwasi heard someone in front of him say, "The gray one."

That meant nothing to him. He turned to Lima and saw him looking back, grim-faced.

"I will go tonight," Queen Nanny said. "We will need to lure one of their pets out of the house and lead him into a trap. It will not be easy, and is likely a suicide mission, but I cannot think of an alternative. I cannot make any of you come with me."

"And we cannot let you go alone," a man near the front said.

His voice was joined by others. "Without you,

we all perish," another said.

It didn't take long. Volunteers made themselves known, standing while others remained cross-legged on the ground. They couldn't have had any idea of what they were letting themselves in for, but there was no denying their bravery.

Kwasi added his voice to the calls.

"I will think on it," Queen Nanny promised. "Now there is work to be done. Firewood to be gathered, food to be caught and cooked. As mundane as it sounds, life does not end just because a few of us may die tonight."

So she sent them to gather food and fuel, while others set about building an additional shelter in the hope more than expectation of others joining them in the coming days. No one said anything about the beds that would be freed up if they failed.

TEN

Nightfall came.

Queen Nanny led the way. They marched through the trees, following a path that Kwasi hadn't walked before. It made him appreciate the sheer size of the wildwood. They could have hidden within its boundaries for months without being found, even if the enemy sent their henchmen in search of the village every day.

He tried to pick out markers that might lead him back if, gods forbid, he was forced to try and make his way back alone. There was precious little to differentiate one tree from another.

The path was clearly well used, but following a dirt track in complete darkness was nigh on impossible at the best of times—and running for your life wasn't ever the best of times. It all came down to survival. Normally, the smart move would be to find somewhere to hide and try and see the night out if he became separated from the others, but nothing was normal about the enemy's pets. If those things could smell him as well as any wolfhound, they'd pick up his fear and sweat and follow it wherever he tried to hide. Seeing the dawn all came down to being on the right side of Queen Nanny's protection.

"This is the limit of our enchantment. Beyond this point, we are vulnerable," Queen Nanny said, pointing to a splash of white on a tree.

It was something, at least. Enough to tell him that he was on the right track if he was lost and alone.

Part of him knew that was sheer optimism. They were walking into a den of beasts and other fell fiends, looking to snare one and get away with it. Anyone in their right mind knew it was nothing short of insanity to even try. The truth was once they were inside the house—if they got that far—it was unlikely any of them would leave, no matter what magics Queen Nanny wielded.

The spear felt impotent in his hand. He would have felt better with a machete, perhaps, or a cutlass.

There were five of them; six, including Queen Nanny. It was their responsibility to keep her out of harm's way—if they could.

At best, they would serve as bait in the hopes of drawing out one of their devil dogs, and once it was on their heels, run like hell itself was on their tail, straight back to where she waited to spring her trap. At worst, they wouldn't make it that far, and the thing would tear them to shreds.

Up ahead, he saw three bodies still hanging from branches.

Mercifully, it was too dark to make out any of their features in the gloaming, but it was obvious that their bodies had suffered terrible damage. He could only pray that the worst of it had happened after death.

He did his best to ignore them, concentrating instead on the house half a mile farther ahead, across the no man's land of plantation soil, downhill from them.

Was it possible to see the bodies from the windows? Did they serve a dual purpose, a macabre entertainment for those who lived in the mansion?

Queen Nanny hadn't talked in any detail about the house, the plantation that lay next to it, or the people who lived behind those white walls. The only thing she had said that Kwasi found interesting was that she had escaped from the place, a long time ago now, and that she had heard tell of the White Witch Kwasi had seen practicing her dark arts in the flesh. "But she is not the same as the enemy," Queen Nanny had said. "For all her evils, she is mortal... she can walk in daylight without fear. She is different, yes, but she is not the enemy's kind. She is her own kind of evil. She lives among them, has something the enemy needs, and for that reason, they accept her."

"Could her magic be the secret to allowing the enemy to walk in daylight?" Lima had wondered, but Queen Nanny hadn't had the answer.

"Did you see anything unusual about the body you found this morning?" Queen Nanny asked.

"This morning?" Kwasi asked, feigning ignorance.

"Don't play foolish games with me, Kwasi. I do not have the patience," she whispered so only he could hear. The others had taken up position along the tree line, keeping watch a few steps away from them.

He shook his head. "She was dead. That's all I saw. Nothing else mattered."

She nodded. "It was the girl who was captured? Your friend?"

He hesitated, unable to maintain eye contact, and scuffed the ground.

"There's no shame," she said. "If you had stayed, you would be dead, too."

This time, he nodded. "It was Afua."

"You saw her again when you went back with Lima?"

Again, he nodded.

"Then the enemy knows who you are, that you are one of us. Nothing they do is accidental. There is reason behind it all: fear. Are you sure there was nothing strange about her body?"

"She was dead. Isn't that strange enough?"

She nodded and let it drop, turning her gaze back to the house. "I'll need you to be seen," she said after a moment. "You've gotten away from them twice. They won't want to let you go again."

"I will be the goat tied to the tree," he said bleakly.

"I hope not. The goat never has the chance to run. All you'll need to do is get back here before their pet catches you."

They waited within the confines of the trees until the last faint glow of the sun had gone from the sky. A few clouds scudded across the moon.

The slight breeze rustled through the trees and set the hanging bodies swinging again, but none of the five uttered a word.

Eventually, far in the distance, they heard a door open, then slam again, the sound carrying across the distance.

"It is time."

The dogs would be released at night to hunt down any slaves foolish enough to try and escape. Kwasi knew from bitter experience that the sound of them prowling outside was enough for anyone in the huts to keep the doors closed.

"I would imagine they will go to the huts first," Queen Nanny said, using reason to try and work through the unreasonable. "They usually do, but not always. There should be time before they come this way. How much, I don't know, even though I have come here to watch them often enough."

That surprised Kwasi. He knew that she'd escaped from this place, but not that she haunted it like a specter. Why would she want to come back and torment herself? Had she left someone behind?

As the thought crossed his mind, Kwasi was forced to admit that he hadn't really thought about Queen Nanny as a survivor like he was and what cost that survival always entailed. All of them had left someone behind somewhere.

He stepped out of the trees without waiting to be told. No one moved to stop him.

He wanted to show himself without moving too far from the protection of the trees. He wanted the things in there to see him. Maybe not on a conscious level, but on a deep, primeval one. He wanted the fight that was to come.

Behind him, he heard Queen Nanny begin her incantations, weaving a magical trap they would need to snare one of the beasts—assuming he would be able to lure it back to her.

He knew the risks. He knew that if one of those human-dogs caught him, his life would be over, but strangely, he didn't care anymore. He was prepared to die if that was the price of victory.

The three others who were armed clutched their sharpened spears. Each had a knife tucked into his belt. Kwasi had neither now. He had planted his spear in the ground before emerging from the woodland. And as much as it might have eased his mind to carry a knife, the truth was, if one of those things caught him, a knife wouldn't help. At best, it would prolong his agony.

He took those first few steps with confidence, but the farther he moved from the trees, the less confident he became and the more resigned to his fate.

By the time he was halfway to the white house, Kwasi wanted desperately to look back, just reassure himself the others were still there. More, though, he wanted to run. The specters of those three poor souls haunted him every bit as much as the ghosts of those six transformed pets curled up in the dirt, dead. He wouldn't look back. He wouldn't run. Either would be showing weakness when he had to be strong.

He stopped and waited.

Listening.

They were out there in the darkness. He could hear them, even if he couldn't see them.

He was at the point of no return. Even a few more strides and it was unlikely he'd win a race back to the trees before one of the beasts caught him.

Every muscle in his body tensed, coiled, ready to spring. His life depended on running like the wind. He knew he was fast, but was he fast enough?

He would find out soon.

And then he saw the shadows moving, halfway between the house and where he stood.

Too close. If they started to run now, he would be dead long before he reached Queen Nanny's snare.

He didn't dare move.

They moved slowly, cautiously, as though unsure what he was.

Don't move, he thought, every ounce of his being concentrated on standing stock-still.

It seemed to be working. He heard them sniffing at the air and the soft, padding footfalls as they walked the line.

Then one of them snarled, and Kwasi knew he couldn't linger even a heartbeat longer. He had to run. Now. With every ounce of strength he had in his body.

He turned and bolted, eyes fixed on the trees where he knew Queen Nanny and the others waited. He couldn't see them. All he could make out were the dark shadows of the swaying bodies still hanging from their ropes. It didn't matter; he trusted the strange woman with his life.

Kwasi ran through the pain, his lungs bursting. On his heels, he heard them, their snarls getting louder.

He pushed himself on, head rolling on his shoulders, fingers clawing at the air, trying to find every precious inch he could even as his legs lost their power, the muscles on fire, quivering, his heart thundering, unable to keep up the frantic pace he'd set himself.

He was a dead man. His mind had already given up.

But his body hadn't.

As one, the three other men emerged from the trees, brandishing their spears, and started to run toward him, howling and hollering to get the beasts' attention.

On the front foot, the first of them launched his weapon, and for one sickening second, Kwasi felt the displaced air as it whistled by, incredibly close to him.

He closed his eyes but didn't stop. The howl behind him told him everything he needed to know: the spear had found its target.

And still, he didn't stop running, because that

spear tip hadn't killed the enemy's pet—it had only slowed the damn creature down.

There were two more on his tail and getting closer with every bound, their huge gait eating the ground between them.

Another spear flew but this time missed.

Another of the men rushed past, spear held out in front of him as though he intended to impale the oncoming beast. He screamed as he ran.

His screams were met by a roar, a growl, and then another scream as a second man joined the fray.

The third stood motionless just a few paces ahead of Kwasi, brandishing a wicked knife.

"Run!" Lima shouted, urging him on, but Kwasi didn't need the encouragement. Huge paws pounded at the dirt behind him. He was sure he could feel the beast's hot breath on the back of his neck.

He kept his eyes focused on the trees, trying

to believe there was actual safety to be found there. He surged past Lima, stumbling those last few yards as he reached the trees.

The beast leaped, the roar filling in his ears. Huge claws gouged at his back as it crashed to the ground.

Kwasi felt the impact shiver through the dirt and was hit by a sudden flood of relief, unable to believe he was safe.

He fell to his knees, gasping for breath he couldn't seem to hold in his lungs, fell forward, then scrambled, spinning around until he sat on the ground, his heels scrabbling against the earth, and kept kicking back to put more distance between himself and the thing.

Queen Nanny stepped between them, her face utterly emotionless, as if carved from the wildwood. The air crackled with bluish-white light that sparked around her fingers as she reached out.

The other beasts were forgotten. All her

attention was devoted to the wounded creature as it howled out its agony, thrashing in the dirt as it struggled desperately to free itself from the snare of magic that held it in place. The light sparked and cackled, sheathing its fur, singing and scorching it.

The enemy's pet was different from the others Kwasi had seen; the fur was streaked with gray rather than black, and its teeth were chipped and cracked and yellowed, but looked every bit as lethal as the others'.

Queen Nanny repeated her incantation, her voice thickening, deepening, tapping into a rich vein of the earth's natural magic.

The beast howled.

She stepped forward, standing over the creature. Now Kwasi saw the sadness in her eyes. She took no pleasure from inflicting so much pain on the pitiful man-animal. He was forced to cover his ears to block out the worst of the creature's pain as it began to change. The

transformation was slow at first, but in a matter
of heartbeats, the writhing, curling, coiled,
twisted shape on the ground became a man.

The pain was no less, but somehow, the beast
managed to find the strength to say, "Thank
you, my heart." The words were barely more
than a whisper, and Kwasi couldn't be sure he'd
heard them for what they really were rather than
applying his own sense of shape to them.

Queen Nanny leaned forward and placed a
hand on his cheek, wiping away a tear. "It will be
over soon, Kosi. Let go, dear heart. Be at peace."

Pain clearly racked him again, his spine
arching more than it had any right to, each bone
rigid.

"Not long," she promised. "But I can't let you
go, not yet... as much as it hurts me to see you in
such pain... I need to know what the enemy are
doing. Tell me, and I can end this, and you will
finally be free of it..."

"Ask," Kosi managed through clenched teeth.

"We know that they have a way to walk in the light, or think they do. What magic is it?"

"The White Witch," he managed before another wave of pain took him and he howled his agony.

Queen Nanny didn't move and took no measure to end his suffering. She simply waited until Kosi could muster the strength to speak again.

"She's taking the blood of our kind... She corrupts it... and gives it to the enemy. I don't know how..."

"Thank you," she said, and this time, she leaned forward and placed a tender kiss on Kosi's lips. When she lifted her head again, his last spark of life had slipped away.

Kwasi saw the blood across Kosi's neck where she had opened a second smile like it was an intimate gift she could bestow. Kwasi hadn't seen the knife work, but he saw the blade in Queen Nanny's hand and knew she had found a way to end the poor man's pain once and forever. He wondered who the man had been to her, as Queen Nanny closed his eyes and ran her fingertips along his cheek. "Goodbye, my love."

ELEVEN

It was only then that Kwasi realized that he didn't hear the others. He looked around but couldn't see them.

Somehow, they must have dealt with the beasts. Now he feared for their safety.

He scrambled to his feet and rushed out past the tree line, finally able to see the dark shapes on the ground: five bodies, but only one of them was sitting upright. He ran toward them, all the pain and exhaustion forgotten.

The two beasts were dead, though they hadn't returned to their natural human. Instead, they were caught in some weird aberration, a half-formed combination of the two; neither one thing nor the other.

Two of the men lay motionless on the ground, their bodies savaged by the beasts before their spear tips had brought them down. Queen Nanny had blessed the steel; it was only her magic that saw the metal slice through that armor-like hide. Only Lima was alive, his eyes glazed over and unfocused as Kwasi knelt before him.

"You will need to carry him back," Queen Nanny said, appearing at his shoulder. "But there are measures that need to be taken here first. Help me to pull these bodies together."

He did as he was asked, dragging the two half beasts together, then laying their fallen comrade on top. Finally, he helped Queen Nanny carry the man she had called Kosi and placed him with tender care on the top. He was considerably lighter than Kwasi had expected, as if the transformation to his true self had caused the bulk of his muscle to waste away.

"You can go now," she said. "Take Lima back, and I will follow in a while. There are things I need to do here first."

Kwasi nodded. He thought about protesting, but she had already turned her back on him.

He helped Lima to his feet, checking him over for injuries. There was a scratch on his face and blood on his shirt, but he didn't complain when he stood up. He didn't appear too badly hurt, but he was barely able to walk, even with help, dazed and confused. He had stood toe-to-toe with one of the beasts and survived. That was more than the other two had managed between them. That spoke volumes about the man Lima was.

Kwasi helped his friend to the trees. They hurried despite the fact there was nothing left to hurry from.

Behind Kwasi, he heard Queen Nanny's voice again. The words were in that tongue he didn't recognize as any language he'd ever encountered, but somehow responded to on a primal level.

A moment later, there was a blinding flash lit the trees ahead of him and a sudden roar chased him.

Kwasi glanced back, afraid of what he might see.

The funeral pyre was ablaze. The bodies were engulfed in flame, with Queen Nanny kneeling close to them.

He lingered for a moment, watching, before feeling that he was intruding on her personal grief. He turned his back on the pyre and carried on walking with Lima until others met them closer to the village. Everyone was desperate for news of what had happened out there on the plantation's edge. The questions came in a babble of voices. Neither one of them answered, though. Hands reached out to take Lima's weight and help share the burden for the last of the walk.

In the shadow of the firelight, Lima told them all, "We will wait for Queen Nanny to return. Then you will have your answers."

None would go against her, so they waited. The firepit in the center of the clearing was more welcoming than the one they had left behind. Kwasi was grateful to slump in front of it, ridding his bones of the deep chill that had taken root.

They waited in silence, listening to the symphony of the night with its wildlife instruments.

Queen Nanny did not rush to return, the funeral pyre burning well into the night. But when she did, with the red morning on the horizon, her face was smeared with ash, and her clothes reeked of a smoke Kwasi would remember for the rest of his life.

She walked to the center of the circle, stooped, and put something in the fire before she returned to her tree stump. A memento from Kosi?

The questions began, though Queen Nanny silenced them with a raised hand and a promise— "In good time"—before she sat and bade they all do likewise.

She closed her eyes, then began to tell them what had happened out there. It was not a pleasing firepit tale, and for Kwasi, who had been there, it was still too raw, especially as she didn't waste words trying to soften the blow of the deaths. There were sobs from the onlookers.

She didn't say anything about Kosi, the man she had freed of the bestial curse, nor her relation to him, and Kwasi had no intention of asking her in front of everyone. If she had wanted to share, she would have. It was enough that the dead man had given Nanny what she had asked for with his dying breath.

When she finished describing the pyre and how she had knelt there with the dead until their souls could travel home, she said, "We don't have long. Our fears are confirmed. Soon the enemy will be able to hunt during the day, and our sanctuary will be in danger. My wardings will be useless under the sun because I am simply not strong enough to maintain them all day and all night. Exhaustion will claim me, and they will come to destroy us. Those they don't kill, they will drag back to their nests. I will be too weak to fight, and no matter how desperately the rest of you do, you will not be able to stop them."

Fear rippled across the faces of the onlookers.

She recounted what she knew about the blood that was being taken and how she was sure the corpses hanging from the trees had been drained for that purpose as much, if not more, as to serve as a message to them. "What I don't know is how much this White Witch needs to fulfil her promise to the enemy or how long it would take for her magic to work on it. But I fear it will not be long before they drink this blood that will change them once and forever, and then we are all as good as dead. We must take the fight to the enemy, and we must do it before they have gathered their strength. As much as I have counseled caution in the past, that means moving against them with haste, lest this White Witch gives them the gift they so crave. We win by killing her."

"And by striking before they can raise more hounds," Kwasi suggested, the words coming to his lips without thought.

Queen Nanny nodded her agreement. "You are right, friend Kwasi," she said. "If we act quickly, we can scupper their plans, and even though we may not be able to get rid of them all, we won't have to. Our focus should be on the White Witch, who has set up home in their nest, and destroy her, and we can deny them the powers they crave, casting them forever in darkness. That is how we defeat them. And if we do not have to fight through a dozen of their pets to get to her, all the better. Gather anything that can be used as a weapon. We will be leaving here before dawn."

No one questioned her. None so much as murmured dissent among themselves. They had been preparing for this moment. They were ready. They would fight. Some would die. But that was as it needed to be. They would fight to the last man and could only pray that would be enough. But even if it wasn't, death was sometimes better.

***

A cry went up from the within the trees, cutting across the sounds of movement and items being retrieved from the huts.

"Tula is awake!"

It was enough to make everyone stop what they were doing. It drew Queen Nanny from her own shelter and set her running through the camp to where Tula had been resting.

The young woman was still caught in the half-life between sleep and wakefulness, her eyes fluttering open only to close just as quickly. Queen Nanny crouched down beside her, gentling her brow as she would a frightened animal, then began to examine her wounds in the burgeoning light while Kwasi held a lamp for her.

He needed to be at the heart of things; he needed to do everything he possibly could to help. It was on him. She was his burden. His guilt. He had done this to her, every bit as surely as if he had sunk his own teeth into her neck.

"She is stirring, but it could still be hours before she is fully awake and free of the malaise," Queen Nanny told him. "But the fever has broken, and that is something. Now we need to wait. We can do no more. It is up to her. She needs to be strong. Pray for that much, at least."

"The gods give her strength," Kwasi said, though it was no sort of prayer. It was a plea to the universe.

Queen Nanny called for the older woman who had been keeping watch over Tula and bid her to carry on with the duty until they returned.

If they returned.

TWELVE

The remains of the five bodies were still smouldering when they reached them. The air was heavy with the sickly-sweet smell of roasting meat.

Kwasi's guts churned in rebellion. He held his breath as best he could until they were well past it. Others in their party could not take their eyes off the horror. He gripped his spear tighter, though he knew the dead posed no danger.

Before they stepped out of the trees, Queen Nanny performed a blessing on their weapons. The men around Kwasi clutched theirs as if they were protection from the evil itself.

The plantation house was now in darkness, save for a lambent glow coming from one of the upstairs windows, a sliver of light like a silver dagger where the drapes weren't completely drawn. If it had not been for that, they could have been fooled into thinking the entire house was sleeping.

Did the people in there have any idea what had happened to their pets just a few hours before? Or were they living in blissful ignorance?

He had no idea what sort of leash they kept their pets on. Did they release them to prowl and not expect them to return—or send someone to recall them—until first light when they have to return to hide away in the darkness like their masters? Even so, surely someone in the house would have seen the funeral pyre and wondered? Or were they so arrogant they just didn't care?

"That's the master's room," Queen Nanny explained. "There are others in there, but he is the real enemy, one of the true evil ones. His death will make the other desperate and unsure. We need to remove him from the field of battle. Cut the head off the beast. With him gone, the others will be desperate and too busy fighting among themselves to understand what is happening to them."

Their plan, such as it was, was no more complex than getting into the house and wreaking as much damage as they could as quickly as possible. With luck, they would add to their supply of weapons in the process. It would be a bonus if they could find and destroy any of the enemy, but that wasn't the main objective. With dawn fast approaching, there was a chance they might get lucky. But before then, they lacked the power to hurt any of them, never mind kill one of their number.

They moved closer to the house, staying close to the shadows. The sunrise was painfully slow, the first blush barely on the horizon.

Kwasi's heart thundered in his rib cage. He was sweating despite the chill in the air.

They took cover, waiting for the blood-red sky to swell with its grave omens.

Kwasi had tried to count how many of them were there. He'd reached thirty but was sure there were others that he couldn't see. Thirty. It was hardly an army. Was it enough to stand against one of the men Queen Nanny had called the enemy? Maybe. But he couldn't imagine the sky would be enough to bring them all down, swollen with portents of bloody slaughter or not.

More weapons weren't the answer, either, not without more people to wield them. If they could free more of their brothers and sisters, that was well and good. Some might even join their fight, but most wouldn't; they would flee and hide and try to find a way off the island. But some would. And maybe they would be enough to make a difference? "Together, we are strong," he muttered under his breath.

Queen Nanny whispered orders, telling a group of them to attempt to force the locks securing several of the slave huts so that any who would join their fight could. The outbuildings were hidden from sight of the main house. Kwasi was pleased that she seemed to be of a similar mind. He offered to accompany them.

"No," she said with a gentle shake of the head. "Stay with me. I need you and Lima close. I want you inside the house with me."

Other groups were dispatched to the other side of the house, while more still were sent to the cottages where the slave masters lived to make sure that they stayed there.

The fewer people they had to confront inside the house, the better their prospects of surviving this fight. Anything they could do to ensure that those numbers did not swell to complicate things would be helpful.

That left less than ten of them standing there, waiting for instructions from Queen Nanny. She did not rush her decision, instead listening for some signal they could not hear. She inclined her head, and for the longest time, it seemed that she did not draw a single breath, until finally Queen Nanny said, "It is time."

The sky had lightened, the blood red spilling

out into the black like a hemorrhage. It would be a while yet before the sun rose above the horizon, but if they left it much later to make their move, the servants and residents of the house would begin stirring.

Only three of them went inside with her, through the front door. The rest had very simple orders: kill any man or woman who came out of the place.

Queen Nanny said, "The enemy are arrogant. They do not believe anyone will stand against them and cannot imagine anyone having the temerity to steal from them. The only bolts thrown at night are on the slave huts, and those bolts are on the outside to keep the slaves inside. Those bolts will be thrown open tonight, just as the front doors of the big house will be thrown wide. This is our moment."

Kwasi took a breath before following her inside. The huge foyer lay in near darkness, with the only light coming in through the open door.

"Leave the door open," she said after the others had entered. "We may need to leave in a hurry."

"Which way?" Kwasi asked.

She was already making for the wide staircase that lay ahead of them. Queen Nanny paused, then looked back. "You, come with me," she told Kwasi. "The rest of you, stay here. If anyone comes down, they don't get to leave the house through any door other than that one." She pointed to the open door.

Kwasi understood. If the dawn was their greatest weapon, then it would be best to lead the enemy into its arms. The others waiting outside would make sure they didn't get far.

"Where are we going?" he asked as she led the way up the stairs.

She touched a finger to her lips. It was a question that didn't need answering. They were going to the only room that had a light burning in its window.

Queen Nanny trod softly, moving through the house like a ghost. Kwasi followed warily, on edge and looking for movement in the shadows. He saw nothing. At the top of the first flight, he paused and glanced back down to see one of the others had taken up position.

"This way," Queen Nanny whispered, turning to the left.

Light bled out beneath one of the doors along the corridor, the only light they had seen since they had come inside. It had to be the master's room; that was what she had called it.

She knew the layout of the house well. How many times had she walked these hallways? He couldn't allow himself to be distracted. He knew that it was his fear worrying away at his mind, looking for weaknesses to make him crumble. If these things were as powerful as Queen Nanny believed they were, then the two of them with simple spears didn't stand a chance against whoever was behind that door, Queen Nanny's magic or not.

Courage was a fleeting thing. But Kwasi didn't need to be brave because he was prepared to welcome death like an old friend.

A scream filled the house, followed by the rapid clatter of footsteps on the stairs.

"Now! Quickly!" Queen Nanny rasped and rushed to the door. She flung it wide open to reveal a room filled with candles.

A young woman lay on the bed, her clothes torn away from her body in strips and stained with a crimson that seemed to be spreading, even in the flickering light.

She wasn't alone. Kwasi saw one of the men he had seen grab Tula. The man's mouth was wide, teeth too large for it to accommodate them, and all down his chin and chest, Kwasi saw blood.

The enemy looked up, eyes bestial, in a blood frenzy. Kwasi saw a moment of recognition in them, but it was fleeting. The enemy's gaze fixed on Queen Nanny, and rage replaced recognition.

He moved toward her, quicker than any man had a right to. Kwasi was half a step slower, but still quick enough to put himself between Queen Nanny and the enemy, his spear leveled in front of him.

A sword stood propped against an upholstered chair beside the bed. The blade was sheathed, and a leather strap hung loosely over the back of the chair.

The fiend glanced at it—barely a flicker of the eye—but made no move toward it.

There was no room for hesitation; Kwasi knew what he had to do.

He closed the gap between them and, with all his strength, drove the tip of the spear into the thing's stomach. He'd expected more resistance, but the metal tip slid in with little effort. The enemy's own momentum took it another half step into the spear, his eyes flaring wide in shock. Kwasi was grateful for the length of the spear's wooden shaft. It kept them apart.

The sound of footsteps drew closer. More people came through the door. Voices cried out, filled with courage and outrage at the sight of the murder happening in front of them and the young woman on the bed.

Two figures rushed in to join Kwasi in the fight, each ramming another spear toward the enemy, who seemed more perturbed than hurt by Kwasi's attack. Their spears didn't stop the fiend.

A knowing smile flitted across his blood-smeared face. And then, inexplicably, the enemy took another step toward Kwasi, the spears plunging deeper through its flesh without pain. Whatever blessing Queen Nanny had given the spear tips didn't seem to be having any effect.

It came on another step, close enough for Kwasi to smell the fetid stench of its breath.

Despite the blood smeared across its face, or perhaps because of it, the enemy's skin had a deathly pallor. Its cheekbones and jaw were both delicate and strong, and its long hair, streaked with white, was cinched back with a leather tie. As dead as its complexion was, its eyes were alive with malice.

Queen Nanny whispered something under her breath, then reached out a hand. Without any seeming strength behind the blow, she pushed the fiend back and sent it staggering with a force Kwasi couldn't imagine her possessing.

The enemy stumbled back, shaking its head like a dog before it came at her again.

Queen Nanny gasped one of the spears protruding from the thing's carcass, barking a sharp command to anyone in the room with the presence of mind to act on it. "Open the drapes! Do not hesitate. I cannot hold him much longer. We need light in here. Light and life!"

One of the two newcomers released his grip on his spear, moving for the drapes. The enemy took another merciless step toward Queen Nanny, one hand reaching out to claw at her face but falling short. Kwasi saw the yellow-pointed talons rake through the air only inches from her face.

There was no stopping it.

They were going to die here—like the young woman on the bed, like Afua, and everyone else who had come before these terrible creatures.

The man snatched at the drapes, frantically pulling them aside. In his panic, he almost tore them from their rail. Fabric ripped and something clattered to the floor. Then the drapes fell from the huge windows, and early-morning light flooded the room.

The effect was instant.

No longer interested in trying to attack Queen Nanny or Kwasi, the enemy fought like a fiend to free itself from the spears that pinned it in place. It thrashed wildly, clawing at the wooden shafts, barely managing a half step backward, which, in all the fighting, had led him closer to the window, not farther away.

There was no mistaking the pain the thing

was suffering. Its actions became increasingly frantic, like an animal caught in a trap. But unlike a wild animal, it knew the consequences of its entrapment.

Kwasi had no sympathy for it. Queen Nanny urged them to push even harder and put an end to its unlife.

The spears sank deeper. The blessed tips were already through the other side of its body.

The enemy staggered back, first one step, then another. The spear tips scratched against the glass.

It didn't understand, even as the scream tore from its bloody mouth. It was a single, ear-splitting shriek that seemed to go on forever and only ended with the crash of glass as the window gave way. Wood splintered, glass cracked, and suddenly, there was no more resistance.

The creature fell back, no longer even the mockery of a man as its flesh smoked and burned, the meat on its bones shrinking and twisting as it fell. It hit the ground with a dull thump, like a bag filled with sand.

Kwasi leaned through the broken window, expecting to see the corpse on the ground below, the three spears still protruding from it, but that wasn't what he saw. Instead of a body, there was little more than a mound of ash in a vaguely human outline that was already beginning to blow away on the breeze. The spears lay on the ground.

"We have to go," Queen Nanny said, sitting on the bed beside the young woman. Kwasi saw her breastbone shallowly rise and fall. She was still alive—barely—somehow.

"There will be others here," Kwasi said. "They need us."

Queen Nanny shook her head. "There isn't time. The enemy's servants will be waking soon if the ruckus hasn't roused them already. Daylight will not protect us from those. I know you want to fight now, but we must choose when we fight our battles and where. This is not the time nor the place. We have wounded the enemy. Now they will know fear, and that isn't something they are used to. Trust me. This was a battle, not the war."

The young woman on the bed released a harrowing cry that split the air, freezing Kwasi to the spot. Her mouth was wide, and there was no sign of the sound abating. No one in the household would be able to sleep through such a scream.

Queen Nanny didn't hesitate.

She snatched up the sword and drew it from its scabbard, swinging the blade through the air. It almost seemed to sing, even above the scream, and in a heartbeat, she severed the young woman's head from her body.

The dead woman slumped back on the bed, quickly staining it crimson, while her head rolled onto the floor, bouncing twice before coming to a halt.

"I thought we were going to save her," Kwasi

said helplessly.

"We did," Queen Nanny replied.

The silence that followed the decapitation was filled with the sounds of movement deeper in the house.

Together, they ran.

THE OLD WORLD: A FORGOTTEN TIME, A FORGOTTEN PLACE
II

There were noises in the night; sounds that took Nanny back to the dark one of the souls she had tried so hard to banish from memory. It haunted her dreams still, and many a night, she had woken in the grips of cold sweat.

It was far from the first time she had heard something prowling around the perimeter without coming close enough to trigger the wards. It was as if the thing knew and kept its distance, only daring to inch closer with every circuit of the village as it learned where was safe to tread.

It was testing the village's defenses. There was no other explanation, seeing how close it could come without triggering the wardings and taking the brunt of the shocks.

Out there in the black, she saw a sudden flash light up the night and heard a gut-wrenching scream followed by a pitiful howl.

Fully awake, Nanny sat up. She had never heard anything like that before.

The elder woman was still by the fire, just as Nanny had left her hours ago. She was laughing softly to herself.

"What was that?" Nanny whispered, still unaccustomed to her own voice.

"That, my girl," said the elder woman, "was the joyous sound of a job well done."

When Nanny looked puzzled, she explained, "The trap you set was sprung, and the creature's pain proves to me just how strong the old ways are in you. I always knew you had it in you, but now, I am sure. You will be so much stronger than I could have dared hope, proving you give yourself to the study of the art. It is in your hands now."

"No, it wasn't the warding. It was a cry of anguish, a shriek of pain."

"It was all three. Your snare has captured one of the ancient enemy's rabid pets. Who knows. Perhaps you have even saved a man's life?"

Nanny thought about that. If the conjurations she had woven out there around the perimeter had stopped one of those creatures from stealing into the village, then she had saved more than one man's life. But she did not correct the elder woman. She felt no pride in her heart.

It didn't matter who had set the wardings, only that they had worked. And that was, perhaps, the most important lesson the elder woman could have hoped to impart.

"You can go back to sleep now, child," she said, though Nanny was sure that she could hear more of those wretched noises coming from the direction of the scream. It wasn't a cry of pain, though. Now it was one of melancholy and sadness.

She settled down on her bed and listened to the plaintive cry until it was little more than a sob and lacked the strength to keep herself from sleep.

First light had barely touched the horizon when the elder woman shook her awake.

"Time to go and see what your trap snared."

"If it's badly hurt... do we have to kill it?"

The elder woman laughed, a gentle sound, not mocking, but more wryly amused. "There'll be no need for any killing," she assured Nanny. "Though there is a chance it might have freed itself, but that's unlikely, though. I still heard it whimpering a while back."

"Are we just going to let it go, then?"

Another laugh, and she told her, "Patience, girl. All in good time."

There were stirrings from a couple of the shelters as they walked toward the source of the sound. Unlike the other wardings set in defense around the camp, whose nature and effect were clear in the weaving of the ward, this one was different. She had done everything the elder woman had told her to: mimicking her words flawlessly, matching her signs with precision, digging her hands into the dirt, repeating the enchantments, feeding off the magic of the land itself. All of it had been done with delicate care, but everything about the trap's conjuration had been carried out with blind faith.

The perimeter they'd marked out barely extended a dozed paces beyond the farthest shelter in any direction. The elder woman had explained that the smaller the circle they marked out, the stronger the defense. Too great a perimeter, too thin a warding. A spell laid down around a single dwelling was infinitely stronger than one surrounding a village. It took considerable talent to be able to lay a warding around an entire settlement. Even as they approached, they couldn't be sure what their magic had captured.

Nanny stayed a step behind her, hearing the sound again. It was a definite sobbing, like a dog whining for attention, but there was a human quality to it. The spell had been cast outside the natural boundary of worn grass that marked their daily walk around the perimeter, but only by another two paces. It was intended to snare anything that passed over it, rendering the intruder immobile.

Before now, they'd caught innocent animals, even snakes that had been unable to escape the magical restraints. The elder woman had simply picked them up and moved them aside. Freed, they'd been able to scurry or slither away without harm.

This time it was different.

While approaching, Nanny was sure she'd never seen anything like the creature half-trapped in shadow. It lay on the ground, barely moving. Whenever a muscle twitched or the fur on its back rippled, a bristle of sparks flared up from the ground to engulf the poor creature. It gave another cry.

Looking at it stretched out, long back arched painfully, in the half light of the dawn creeping through the canopy, she would have guessed it was some breed of dog, but a real beast of a thing, larger than anything she had seen before. Its coat was stained with dark patches of blood that had dried into the fur. There was no way of knowing how long it might have been there. The poor animal smelled ripe, touched with the stench of rot she associated with death and decay.

The animal pulled against the invisible restraints but couldn't break them. The snare held it pinned to the ground.

"Take a good look at it," the elder woman said, her voice low. "You need to be able to recognize the enemy's pets for what they are, should you ever encounter one again."

She moved aside and let Nanny step forward, walking slowly around the thing.

Despite its captivity, Nanny felt the need for distance, not trusting the magic to hold. She couldn't bring herself to look at the animal's face while walking around it three times, but she wasn't going to turn her back on it until she had. So she swallowed her fear and crouched beside it. She reached out to tilt its head up toward her, but hesitated, unable to make contact.

In her mind, she'd already made the connections and knew it was more than an oversize dog and less than human. But she was having trouble coming to terms with the reality of it. Rather than the purely bestial creature she'd imagined, the wretched thing's face was more like a man. And there was a sadness in its eyes.

"What is it?" she asked, finally turning away.

"I told you. It is one of their pets," the elder woman said. "A creature they send to do the killing when they do not wish to sully themselves. This wretched thing wasn't out here by choice. It didn't savor the hunt. It was forced to venture out, and even now, it is desperately struggling to follow its master's imperative, the demand that it come home despite the fact it cannot free itself. Had this been a normal trap, it would have chewed into its own leg to be free."

The thing strained again and released another whimper.

"What are you going to do with it?"

"Me? I'm not going to do anything. It falls to you, child. It is your trap. You wove the warding. Only you can follow the path to resolve it. But that involves choices. You will have to choose."

"What choice do I have? You said that we weren't going to kill it, so we must let it go. Or do you intend to leave it to die here? Is that it?" She could not believe that the person who had cared for her for so long could be so cruel to any living creature. Kill, yes, in self-defense or out of mercy. But torture? Deliberately see it suffer? No.

"If we let it go, it will return, wiser, and won't be so easily snared."

"Then what I should do? Tell me."

A protective arm wrapped across her shoulder and pulled her in tight, reassuring her. "All you have to do is follow my instructions, child. All will be well. You have my promise."

The elder woman's hands described a complex series of movements in the air, weaving the warding out of the stuff of nature itself, for that was the essence of her power, Nanny knew. She was attuned to the world and the elements, drawing upon ancient powers long since forgotten by most men. There were no components, no powdered old bones, nothing that could be stolen or harnessed. This was the land itself, and the elder woman was merely a conduit. There was powerful magic in the land, the oldest and most noble. It was the magic that had given birth to life and the kind of elemental power that was not to be handled carelessly.

The ritual was unfamiliar, but that came as no surprise. Nanny was still a neophyte when it came to these ancient arts, no matter how many years she studied at the elder woman's feet. There was so much to know and so much she would never know because time would deny them. That was the way with wisdom: it was lost through the generations, with each new one forced to find their own to replace what was lost.

Some of the spells Nanny had seen cast were variations on a similar theme, with similar intentions. This one was different, and she had no idea of what it was intended to achieve. Was it going to release the creature somehow? Or was it going to break the invisible leash its master had on it and make it answer to a different master? Or mistress? Or something else entirely?

Nanny mirrored the movements and repeated the incantations, careful to mimic them to perfection and without hesitation.

She felt the thrill of it, the coursing of raw, elemental power surging up through the ground at her feet, thrilling through her skin and bone, and threw shapes into the air, mirroring the elder woman's hands when she gave the nod. At the very last, she reached down with her left hand— the left hand of dark magic, the elder woman had called it, and the left hand of the old gods, too— and grabbed up a fistful of dirt that she tossed into the air. The grains of black earth fizzled and crackled against the remnants of her previous spell.

The creature cried out, its pain obviously intensifying. Part of her cried with it, but she couldn't allow herself to doubt what she was doing. So she tried to block out the sound and concentrate on what needed to be done.

As the invocation progressed, the creature became even more agitated, fighting harder against the bonds of magic holding it. She realized an aspect of the new spell had reached a point of repetition she recognized; either something wasn't working and it had to be done again, or it needed strengthening. The creature was proving considerably harder to deal with than anything she had fought before.

And then, without warning, the fight seemed to disappear from it.

The elder woman urged her on. Nanny was as tired as she had ever felt, but she couldn't stop—dared not stop—until she was told otherwise. She felt her strength failing, feared she wasn't strong enough in the old magics, and forced herself to draw on inner reserves, biting down on her own pain.

And slowly, the creature began to change.

She was sure it was her imagination, but there was some almost imperceptible difference to the thing. Maybe it was just the color of its coat, or maybe the shape of its eyes, but with each repetition, the changes slowly became more noticeable until, eventually, the thing curled up on the ground was no longer the same creature it had been when they had arrived.

Gone was the dog or wolf. The blood-matted

fur had disappeared and left behind a man lying on his side in the dirt, naked and clearly petrified.

She continued to speak the incantation, the words coming to her lips now as if there were no others she could ever speak. They kept coming until a hand was laid softly on her arm.

"You can stop now, child. It's over. You freed him," the elder woman said. "You've broken the enchantment that bound him in that form. He is free. You did that for him."

Tentatively, the man raised his head from the ground. He looked down at his hands where they pressed into the dirt. They were no longer the paws of a beast, but the hands of a man.

He did not move for the longest time, but then slowly began to rise. Nanny turned her head away, suddenly embarrassed by his nakedness.

The elder woman was unfazed by his body in all its glory, though as far as Nanny knew, she had never known the company of a man. She unhooked one of the layers of cloth from around her waist and handed it to him. "Cover yourself, for the child."

The man held the wrap tightly around him, shivering although the air was already growing warm. The elder woman offered him a drink from a small, stoppered bottle.

"Thank you," he rasped, his voice dry from disuse.

Nanny wondered if his had been as unused as her own. There were so many questions that she wanted to ask, so much she felt she needed to know, but this was not the time. The man was distressed and disorientated. She had no desire to make it worse for him.

"Better?" the elder woman asked, and the man nodded happily, reluctant to let go of the bottle until he was sure that there was no more to come out of it. "Where are your people?" she asked.

"Gone," he said, his voice still gritty, but the words required less effort now.

"Gone where?" Nanny asked, receiving a look of rebuke from the other woman.

"Dead or taken," he said.

"Taken where?" Again, Nanny couldn't hold her tongue. "By the men?"

He shook his head, and his eyes seemed to go out of focus like he was about to swoon and fall. They helped him lay back down again, keeping his head cushioned from the hard ground.

"Not them," he managed. "Though I wish they had. No... it was a different enemy... The devils in the darkness."

The elder woman nodded, but Nanny didn't understand yet. But she would, because this was the fight she was inheriting, where the old blood was all.

The devils in the dark.

The man spoke again, somehow finding the strength, even though his body was failing him.

"They will come for you all," he said. Not a threat. A promise. "Eventually, they will come for everyone. There is no denying them. They will drink your blood to satiate their hunger, or, if you are lucky, they will turn you into something like me, a pet. Either way, death would be better. But only the luckiest get to die."

The next breath he drew rattled in his chest, and each one that followed was more labored than the last. By rights, he should have been dead already, but he clung to life. Nanny didn't waste the moment with questions, despite the hundreds swarming inside her like angry wasps.

"They fear nothing save for the light of day," he said. "They come in the night, shrouded by darkness. The night they took me, they slaughtered most of my village. Only a few of us were taken, and we thought we were the lucky ones until they got us back to their nest. It was a dark and damp place. I don't know what they did to us there, but it changed us. I awoke as the beast you saved me from, and no matter how desperately I fought to be me, to resist them, I was unable to. Whatever they bade me do, I was compelled to do, all the way into death itself if needs be."

"Rest easy," the elder woman said, placing a tender hand on his forehead.

The man flinched despite the gentleness of the gesture, but slowly began to relax, his eyes closing. His breathing grew shallow, as if he was falling asleep, and then it stopped.

"He's at peace now, child. You did a good thing."

"I... I... I..."

"No, believe me, you didn't kill him, if that's what you're thinking. You drove the infection out of him, and that meant he could slip away into the death that had been denied him by the enemy."

Nanny was unconvinced. But hadn't he said himself, death was better?

"I am sure you are drained after the strains of the day," the elder woman said, but before

Nanny could protest, she was given a look that told her she would brook no argument. It was rare that she tasted the other woman's anger and had no desire to do so again. She was tired. The conjuring had been more demanding than any she had attempted before, and not merely because it was of the duration or seemingly endless repetitions. An hour abed in her cot would be welcome.

She retreated into their shelter, pushing her way to the back where her simple bed waited, and settled down. Exhausted, she slipped into a dream-filled sleep.

In those dreams, she relived that night from so long ago when she had hidden while others lost their lives. In this dream, she finally saw the creatures that had attacked them for what they were: beasts like the thing she had snared in her trap. Beasts that, in death, became men, like the one who lay unbreathing only a short way from where she slept.

But there had been something else lurking in the shadows, hadn't there?

Something that had kept out of sight.

When she woke, her body was covered in a sheen of sweat. She went in search of the elder woman and final answers to her most burning questions.

"This enemy," Nanny asked upon finding her, "they turned him into that beast?"

"They did."

"How? What are they?"

"You ask how, not why? That is interesting to me. But, as with all things, you must be patient, girl. There are things about this world you are not yet ready to learn. Content yourself that you did a good thing today and, without doubt, could do it again without me to watch over you if the need arose.

"But we cannot stay here. The threat is too great to us, especially as we have shown our hand to the enemy. They know where we are now. It is only a matter of time before they send more of their pets to hunt us. We must be vigilant and increase the defenses that we set come nightfall. There will be a time, soon, when I will no longer be able to protect these people."

"But you have years ahead of you," Nanny said.

"Perhaps," the elder woman replied, but Nanny knew she was being humored. "But there is nothing written that we will walk them side by side. We need to further your education. First, you must learn how to harness the raw, elemental magic of the earth. It is not as easy as mixing some powders or praying to old bones, like certain priests would have you believe. This goes deeper and means understanding where the old magics reside and how to draw them forth. There are many invocations and incantations you must engrave on your heart, including dark magics I have kept hidden from you until now. You must learn them all."

Nanny nodded.

Magic was not something her guardian lied about. Ever. If she did not want her to know something, she merely told her that she was not ready, and Nanny accepted it. That was the way.

THIRTEEN

Kwasi and Queen Nanny were beyond exhausted when they reached the village.

The others had already returned. Panicked by the sound of the breaking window, they had abandoned their stations and run as one of the overseers, roused by the noise, had come stumbling out of his cottage, firing his gun blindly into the semidarkness.

That single gunshot had woken others. But it took time to react to the confusion, to understand, and to act, and by the time the second shot had sounded, the raiders were escaping, even if they were empty-handed.

The group Queen Nanny had dispatched to free some of their fellow slaves had fared a little better in that they had managed to open one of the huts and, with the meager light of early dawn spilling into the stinking cabin, saw four frightened faces. Two of them grabbed their few possessions they considered precious and followed their liberators, but the two others refused, so great was the fear of the enemy. The sound of the gunshot did not change anyone's mind.

Kwasi had imagined an exodus, all the slaves liberated and running to their freedom, but the reality was more heart-breaking and showed just how much hope had been crushed. It broke something inside him. The two who had taken their chance at freedom had only replaced the two men they had lost to the enemy's guard dogs. It would take more than this. They may have killed one of the fiends, but he'd seen how that thing was immune to their spears and how it hadn't bled when the blades had sunk deep. Its life was so unnatural. Indeed, looking in that thing's eyes, he didn't think of it as life at all, rather the opposite—unlife. It had taken everything they could muster to bring the beast down, and even then, it had been the sunlight that had saved their skins, not Queen Nanny's magic or blessed weapons. And that was just one of them. He'd been at the party. He knew how many of them there were and what it would take to stand against them all.

It was a fight they couldn't win.

But that didn't mean it wasn't a fight worth fighting.

It had already been a long night. It promised to be a considerably longer day. He needed to sleep, but with so much adrenaline coursing through his veins, sleep was never going to come easily. When it did, it would be absolute, his body crashing from the climb down. He couldn't get the memory out of his mind's eye of the thing flailing as it fell through the window, its vile, yellowed claws slashing at his face and those blood-smeared teeth. He lay on his cot for a while, eyes open because the alternative promised nightmares, and rested his body if not his mind.

It was hard to believe any of them were safe, but Queen Nanny had promised the enemy was powerless in daylight. For now, at least, but for how much longer? A night, a week? A month? How close was the White Witch to breaking the stranglehold the daylight had on them?

Outside, people moved around, treading quietly, speaking softly, as they carried out their chores. It was a melancholy silence, more than simple sadness. They were in mourning for those who hadn't come home.

The weight fell away from his bones, and for a while, at least, he was left feeling light-headed, as though his soul had left his body and the flesh that remained bound to the earth was an empty vessel. It was akin to a religious state, but Kwasi was a nonbeliever these days, or at least had no faith in this new God. He had not abandoned the Old Ones of his homeland, in the same way he knew they would never abandon him in this new world, even if they were so far away. He found himself praying to them with a fervor he hadn't mustered in a long time.

He heard no answers, but when did the gods ever deign to provide obvious ones? They weren't the ones given to communing through burning bushes or talking serpents. Their answers would come in the form a victory.

Kwasi eventually abandoned his search for rest, rolled off the cot, and left his shelter. He wandered throughout the village, seeing the young woman they had rescued dressed in borrowed clothes, helping with the chores along with the other women. It made his heart sing. For all the loss these people had suffered, for all the pain they had endured, here she was, living proof their gods hadn't abandoned them in this place. This was the victory he had needed to see. His prayers had been answered, even if he hadn't known what he had been asking for when he had tapped into the divine. She was whole. Indeed, it was as if nothing had happened to her.

Kwasi watched her in silence, unaware that Lima had moved up beside him.

"She was beyond lucky, that girl," the other man said. "Somehow she has shaken off the blood fever, and it seems there are no ill effects."

"Queen Nanny's arts are strong."

"That they are, but it is nothing short of a miracle."

"Then we should thank the gods for their intervention, my friend. Has she said anything that might help us?"

Lima shook his head. "She woke with no idea of where she was or how she got here. She can't remember a thing beyond being brought from one of the huts and taken into the big house. After that, nothing."

"Nothing?"

Lima shook his head. "We both know that is a mercy."

It was hard to fathom how the woman could be there in front of them, relatively unharmed, even to the extent that her mind had blocked out the horrors of that place to protect her. Lima shrugged. He had no answers.

Kwasi watched as she worked. She kept her head bowed and did not speak to the other women, even when they spoke to her. She did as she was asked without question, always with her head bowed, and remained in the leeward shadow of one of the shelters.

"There's something strange about her," Kwasi said after a moment. It was in all the small things, but without knowing what she had been like before, it was hard to say if she was different or if she had always been so diffident and subdued. But, from their brief exchanges, he didn't think so. Tula had struck him as a brave soul, not a mouse.

"You would be changed, too," Lima said. "You know the things they did to her in there, but what you don't know is the cost of Queen Nanny's ministrations, bringing her back. There is always a cost. It is only natural that she is changed. She has defied death itself."

Kwasi wanted to argue with him. Surely, she hadn't been in there long enough for them to have done such soul-breaking things to her, but he was sure she wasn't the same woman who'd gone inside.

The day wore on, the sun slowly crossing the sky to eventually sink behind the trees, until the day was all but spent and it was time for them all to eat together.

There was a somberness about the village. While there hadn't exactly been a sense of jubilation earlier, there had been a sort of grim satisfaction that one of the enemy had fallen. Now, though, with darkness gathering on all sides, there was a growing uneasiness and tension as the unremitting passage of time saw day into night and, with it, the knowledge that they were going to have to do it all over again. It weighed on them.

For this time, the enemy would be ready.

Tonight promised to be infinitely more dangerous than last night.

And Queen Nanny knew that, which was why she rose to address her people, assuring them, "We do not go out again tonight. I will set the defenses as usual, and we will post a watch. But no one is to leave the boundaries of our protection. Is that understood? The risks are too great. We do not want to gift the enemy an easy victory. We must be smarter than them at every turn. They are arrogant and unused to resistance. We must turn that to our advantage, and that means focusing on our strengths as much as trying to exploit their weaknesses. To do the same again is to deliver ourselves to them, like cattle to be bled."

There were murmurs of agreement. "So what do we do?" a voice asked.

"We rest while we can. We do not know the next time we will have the luxury."

"We do nothing?"

"Oh no, far from nothing."

They ate in near silence after Queen Nanny told them what she intended for the night, turning the meal into a council of war. There was a noticeable lightening in the mood. They were not going to sit by idly and wait for the enemy to pick them off one by one. She had other ideas.

Kwasi watched Tula carefully, trying to work out what it was that unnerved him about her. There was something missing, some spark that had gone from her eyes.

When she had eaten, she slipped away, returning to her shelter. When he walked past an hour later, he could hear the soft sound of her sleeping and tried to banish all the dark thoughts he found himself having.

She was alive.

His actions had saved her. That had to be a good thing.

Had to be.

FOURTEEN

At some time during the night, she left.

She hadn't taken anything with her; she had simply risen from her bed and walked out of the village, following a path through the trees without the need of a guiding light and without being seen by any of the watchers Queen Nanny had put on lookout. She hadn't triggered any of the defenses, either, because she had been leaving, not trying to sneak in. She could have been gone minutes or hours by the time one of the women had gone in to check on her and found her cot empty and raised the alarm.

"We must find her," Queen Nanny said without needing to say why it was so vital they did. "If she's nearby, we bring her back here... She cannot return to the enemy."

All eyes turned to Kwasi as he said what they were all thinking. "She's one of their pets now, every bit as much in their control as those things we had to kill."

Queen Nanny nodded. "I failed her, yes, and in doing so, damned poor Tula. I failed to drive their poison from her veins. I don't know whether to pray there's still some little part of her alive in there or if she's gone, as both promise different kinds of torment for her."

"Her bed was still warm," the woman who'd found it empty said.

"Then perhaps she hasn't gone far. There is a chance she will not be able to breach the boundary of our protective barrier without leaving a trace. Find her if you can. Kill her if you have to."

It was a painful order to hear, but to a man, woman and child they trusted that Nanny understood what needed to be done, and would not guide them wrong, no matter the price that had to be paid. And that included Kwasi.

They split into small groups to hunt, each

heading in different directions and following well-walked tracks that would lead to the different plantation houses that had become the enemy's nests.

In the end, it was not much of a hunt. They had barely gone a few hundred yards beyond the wardings before Kwasi caught a glimpse of color and understood what he was seeing. He called for Queen Nanny. Then he rushed ahead, Lima a few paces behind him, while Queen Nanny lingered, crouching on the ground, her fingertips lingering over the dirt where she set their defenses each night, apparently studying it for signs of weakness.

Tula was already well on her way to the plantation house, compelled to return to the same door where she had emerged just moments after the enemy had bitten her. She walked slowly, unsteadily, lurching from foot to foot as she stumbled on, obviously finding it difficult to put one foot in front of another. But if they were going to stop her, they were going to have to move fast. Once she was free of the trees, bringing her down entailed so much more risk.

Kwasi didn't hesitate. She was his guilt to carry. He sprinted after her while Lima ran back to tell Queen Nanny.

Despite the crowding of the trees, his legs soon found a familiar, easy, loping stride as he wove a path among them. He kept his eyes on the woman in the moonlight, closing the distance between them fast, but not fast enough. She was going to make it out of the trees before he reached her.

The temptation was to hurl his spear at her back—to be free of it so that he could run faster as much as to try and bring her down—but he remembered the way the enemy had been oblivious to pain as he'd skewered it in that upstairs room. He knew it wouldn't slow her and would leave him empty-handed if any of the enemy's other pets found him in the dark.

As if the very thought had conjured it, he saw a dark shadow moving out from the shelter of the house, covering the ground quickly as it rushed toward Tula. It seemed to shift in shape and size as it moved, growing with each loping stride.

And all he could think in that moment was if the thing reached Tula before he did, it would be too late to help her. Until that moment, he hadn't realized he still harbored even a faint hope of somehow saving her again.

He hadn't learned.

There was no saving anyone.

Not anymore. Not in this horror-infested new island world.

He ran, calling Tula's name over and over. There was no need for silence. The enemy had already scented her.

She didn't offer any kind of response. She just continued to stumble forward.

The shape shifted again, slowing as it coalesced into the silhouette of a man. He continued to walk into the moonlight, and where the silver fell, Kwasi saw a face he recognized. It was the slave master who had watched when he had been beaten, enjoying every moment, every crack of the whip, every slice and bite into his flesh and each cry of pain.

The man let Tula stumble past him without giving her a glance. He didn't care about her. He was staring into the trees straight at Kwasi.

Kwasi slowed his run sufficiently to be able to launch his spear, channelling all the anger he had into it, then picked up his pace again before the weapon reached its target and pulled out his knife, ready to fight with rage-fueled frenzy to bring the enemy down. The knife was too humble to match Queen Nanny's assault with the sword the night before, but that would not stop him from trying.

The thought coalesced inside his head in the same heartbeat it took for the spear to pierce the thing's arm and pass through, skidding into the ground while the enemy stood there, amused and unhurt.

Kwasi held his knife out like it was a snake about to strike and rushed those last few paces between them. But as fast as he was, someone else was faster, and metal flashed and whistled through the air a step before he joined battle with the enemy. It took him a moment to realize it was Queen Nanny, brandishing the same sword she had used the night before. Somehow, she had overtaken him, and she was barely out of breath as she launched her own blistering attack. Everything about her movements was controlled and aggressive, yet precise, skilled, and deadly. She cut the overseer down, opening a gaping wound that unspooled his guts.

"Go," she said between gritted teeth, and he understood.

He rushed after Tula. She couldn't be allowed to reach the nest. He had to stop her.

Tula stumbled on now, skirts up, clutching

at the fabric with dirty hands that seemed to be caked with thick mud.

A pool of pale light came from the open doorway. It cast a deathly pallor over her face as he reached out to grab her.

Tula stopped, not resisting his pull, and turned to face him. There was no recognition in her eyes.

She leaned closer, her face moving toward his as if about to kiss him. Too late, he realized there was something horribly wrong with it all.

She opened her mouth, bloodless lips smiling as she leaned in close enough to feel the cold of her breath on the skin of his throat, then slammed her jaws shut, teeth snapping closed barely a hair's breadth from the veins of his throat.

Horrified, Kwasi slammed the flat of his hand into her chest and sent her stumbling backward.

She turned to face the open doorway, drawn like a brainless moth to its light. They were less than half a dozen steps from the door. If she walked through it, he failed everyone. Again.

Kwasi scrambled on, but in a blur of movement, Queen Nanny was beyond him. As Tula tried to bite her, she offered Kwasi a chilling glimpse of her razor-sharp incisors that were too long in her mouth.

Queen Nanny welcomed the move, somehow managing to slam her blade in past Tula's teeth and drive it deep into her mouth. She gave a grunt and pushed, ramming the blade in deeper still, until the silver metal protruded from the back of Tula's neck. With a savage twist, she severed Tula's spinal cord. Despite the ferocity with which Queen Nanny had worked blade, it was the sight of Tula's wide and staring eyes—and was that gratitude he saw in there?—that stuck in Kwasi's mind.

Queen Nanny yanked the blade free, and Tula's legs, unable to support her weight, betrayed her.

The sword swung again. This time, Queen Nanny sliced through her neck as she had done with the other woman before, taking three blows to cut cleanly through and sever Tula's head from her body.

The head hit the ground at Queen Nanny's feet while the body staggered back, seeming to live on for a few mindless steps before it, too, fell.

Queen Nanny bent down, snatching up Tula's head by the hair, and turned away from the house.

"Hurry," she said. "We need to get out of here before more of them come pouring out of that infested nest."

Kwasi didn't need telling twice.

Queen Nanny ran beside him, sword still in hand. They started back in the direction of the hillside and the trees that offered the illusion of safety. And it really was no more substantial than that. Had Tula made it back inside the house, they would have been running for their lives with nowhere to hide. The difference between life and death came down to those fine margins. A few strides. That hair's breadth between her bite and Kwasi's flesh.

But they had struck twice now. Surely the enemy would not allow them to strike a third time without brutal retaliation.

The thought of what that might entail chilled his blood.

He snatched up his spear as he ran past the body of the slave master and picked up his pace, eyes on the trees, not sure he would ever feel safe again.

FIFTEEN

Each and every one of them had driven their bodies to the point of exhaustion, but the adrenaline still coursing through their veins meant they were too wired to sleep.

Queen Nanny checked her wards to be sure they held firm and, confident nothing would make it through the woods in their wake, ordered the fire be built up.

The wood fizzed and crackled, each snap like the demented cackle of a hag. The faces around the fire looked as bloodless as if the enemy had sunk their razor-sharp teeth into their necks. A few had retreated to their cots, but most had gathered around the fire, eager to hear Queen Nanny's words.

Kwasi watched as she walked to her usual place, carrying Tula's head by its hair. The dead woman's face swung with her gait. It was a dark thing to behold.

Queen Nanny had fashioned a support frame from three slim branches. They skewered deep into the ground, bound together where their ends crossed to create a cradle at the top. She placed the head in the cradle before stepping back.

He watched as, with her delicate, bony fingers, she began weaving patterns in the air that drew together the ancient magics of the land, summoning them to serve her. The more deft the movements, the more substantial the warding she conjured, it seemed to him.

Without a word to those watching her, she cast one warding after another at the head, muttering incantations, her voice fierce. Kwasi understood barely a handful of the words, but it seemed as if she was calling for something to come to her. He had no idea whom she was attempting to commune with or what she hoped to achieve from her magics, but like the others he watched, enthralled.

In a strange way, it was a memory of home, more vivid than anything else he had witnessed since he had been forcibly taken from it, and that made it all the more chilling to behold as he began to understand Queen Nanny's true nature.

As he watched, the head's skin tone changed, darkening despite the lack of blood.

And then the eyes opened.

The watchers gasped. Whispers spread through them.

They understood what Queen Nanny had done: she had forced a semblance of life inside Tula's head once more.

But at what cost?

She stood there, face-to-face with the head, asking her question after question. More than once, she was forced to reprise the chant she had used to wake the dead, but there were no answers. Tula's dead eyes stayed open, but her lips refused to part. She would not speak.

"It's futile." Queen Nanny sighed, her chin

slumping onto her chest as her head went down. The effort had left her completely drained. "You should rest while you can. There is nothing to be learned tonight."

One by one, her followers returned to their shelters. The fire began to dwindle, blackened wood crackling, sparks drifting up on the column of smoke as it slowly collapsed.

Kwasi was one of the last to go, reluctant to leave her alone with the stubborn head. But eventually, he took to his cot and lay there in silence, listening to Queen Nanny still softy mumbling her incantation. He feared she would continue all night without success because she was too stubborn to give up. As long as she felt there was hope she might break the dead woman's will, she would continue.

As the last of the voices fell silent, he strained to hear her, not because he wanted to but because he had the sound in his head and could not shut it out. He felt compelled to listen, catching the rhythm of the chant until it finally stopped some time just before dawn.

He convinced himself that he must have fallen asleep, but in those moments in the between times, he could have sworn he heard another voice answering Queen Nanny's questions, though he could not make out what either of them said.

He rolled off the cot and edged closer to the open doorway, moving as silently as he could.

The fire had burned down. There was little more than a glow of embers in the firepit. Queen Nanny sat cross-legged, exactly as she had been when he had left her. The only difference—and surely it was his dreaming mind—was that Tula's head was talking to her.

"Tell me, where are the enemy gathering next?" Queen Nanny asked.

"Just as last week," Tula's head said, though there was a pain in her voice, as if what Queen Nanny was doing did not come without a cost.

"The same rooms."

There were more questions, pushing for details for the time of the gathering, who would be in attendance, but the information meant nothing to Kwasi. Still, he listened, horrified and captivated at once, and struck by just how little he knew about the world of the island and the plantation he'd worked.

"What name? Tell me... who is the sacrifice to be?"

"Sacrifice? There is no sacrifice..." Tula's head said.

But Queen Nanny wasn't satisfied with the answer, so she asked her question again and again until the head released an embittered cry that should have woken the rest of the sleepers. "I don't know! They kill who they want to kill!"

The scream went on and on, crying itself hoarse, until the head suddenly fell silent and Tula's eyes closed.

It was impossible to know if Queen Nanny

was satisfied with the answers she'd been given, but she seemed content to let the dead stay dead rather than spend more of her life force trying to claw Tula's spirit back from that other place.

She picked up the head from its resting place on the frame and knelt to place it almost tenderly in the remains of the fire. The embers burst into life. Flames licked the blackness of the night, and the sickly sweet stench of burning hair and flesh filled the air.

Kwasi was still thinking about what he had seen when he finally drifted back into a fitful slumber filled with dark dreams.

The corpses still hanging from branches in the tree line spoke to him as he walked toward them, each of them blaming him for what had happened. But he kept walking because he had to until he found Afua, her body drenched in blood, the wound at her neck gaping wider than it had before.

"I miss our homeland," she told him, her voice

filled with such sadness. "I should have run faster, but you should have rescued me. You should have helped me escape before they brought us to this place." She fell silent.

"I'm sorry. I'm so very, very sorry," Kwasi said, his dream words barely above a whisper.

She looked at him then, no love in her dead eyes. "This is your fault. All of this."

He woke in a cold sweat with the first light of dawn beginning to fill the clearing.

He knew that he ought to try to go back to sleep, but he never wanted to sleep again. Not if Afua was waiting for him in his dreams. It hurt too much.

SIXTEEN

"The dead spoke last night," Queen Nanny intoned, giving due weight to her words. She had called them all together. "Though not the words we had hoped to hear. When I was alone with Tula's skull, she spoke. I say, 'Tula,' but it was not her. It is a mistake to think of that thing as the woman who lived with us. She is long since gone. This was an agent of the enemy. It knew things only the enemy could know."

"But can you believe it, then?" The question came not from Kwasi, but from another, though it could have been plucked clean out of his head.

"I don't know. The dead can lie every bit as convincingly as the living. But she fought so hard not to speak, I choose to believe. There is still so much we do not know about these things and what happens to good people when they are infected by the enemy." She paused for a moment to make sure that she had everyone's attention, but of course she did. They were hanging on her every word.

The fire was no longer burning, but the head still lay in the ashes with the charred remnants of wood that hadn't been consumed. The air was already feeling warm and filled with the sound of insects. It was going to be another hot day, but none of that mattered.

Queen Nanny continued. "It told me where that the next gathering of the enemy will take place."

She named the house, but the name meant nothing to Kwasi. When he looked around, he saw a similar lack of recognition on most of the other faces, though a couple of people nodded.

"There will be a sacrifice this coming night, which makes me fear the White Witch's schemes are coming to fruition. Will she succeed? I do not know... and care less to guess, but we must assume she will and that she will liberate the enemy from the shackles of the darkness. And for that reason alone, we cannot allow her to proceed. We must do everything we can to stop her."

There were mumbles of agreement. It was impossible not to sense the tension among the gathering.

"But there can be no denying that bringing her down will be beyond dangerous for anyone going near that house. And should we fail, then even those who remain behind are at risk, as is every living soul on the island. I say this White Witch must be stopped, whatever the cost to us."

For a long moment, there was only the distant sound of birds.

Kwasi knew that he would go with her and any of the others who would join them, but he recognized the look on some of the faces around him. Of course he did. He had felt it stir deep inside his gut but named it now for what it was: fear.

"I will fight," Kwasi said, getting to his feet,

with Lima doing the same only a fraction of a second after him.

In less than half a minute, most of them were on their feet, even the old and the infirm, some who were barely able to stand. They were united in this, against the enemy. There were a few who did not stand, but not because of fear for themselves, though; they clutched young children close to them. But even with the majority on their feet, it was not that many.

Not enough.

They needed more time to grow their numbers, raiding night after night to free other slaves, convincing them to join their resistance, but they were out of time.

Queen Nanny motioned for them sit again, but it was obvious she was moved by them.

"Four days. No more. That is the most we can risk. The next gathering is too soon for us. We do not have the weeks we need. Nothing matters now beyond Saturday night. We do not have the luxury of time to waste on gathering fuel and food to last us beyond that. If we survive, then having hungry bellies will be a small price to pay."

She told them what they would need to do, gathering volunteers for key objectives in the coming fight and assigning duties. They gathered what weapons they had: spears, a few knives, and, of course, the sword that Queen Nanny had used to such chilling effect. It did not take any great wisdom to see that they were lacking, so she ordered some to craft more spears, as many as they could.

Even so, Kwasi doubted that there could ever be enough. They had shown they could take the fight to one enemy, but two, three, a dozen? Going against them all at once, with no more than these few tools of death, made his heart sink. They were going to die. They all knew it, and yet they still lined up to go into battle for her. Did they think Queen Nanny had some great, secret magic in her arsenal? Something she could conjure that could drain the deathless blood from those walking corpses?

All he knew about himself was that he would rather die fighting rather than waiting for death to come and find them all cowering.

He turned to Lima. "Promise me, if they take me, you will not let them make me into one of their pets."

The other man nodded solemnly. "Likewise, brother. We die but once. You have my word. The enemy be damned, they won't take either of us."

"We will need firewood," Nanny said at last. "If we cannot bring the sun to them, we can at least bring its fire."

IN THE LAIR OF THE WHITE WITCH
II

The dogs were running; that was what the Others called the abominations that had once been slaves and now barely functioned as pets. It was the Mistress who had shown them how to mutate the slaves.

The Others secreted their own infections through their bite, spreading the unlife through the wounds their teeth opened. Something in their bodily fluids spread the death in the veins of their victim—and, if they accepted the gift, did so without killing them. These gets were in their thrall. The Others had control over them as their sires.

What she had shown them went beyond a simple siring. She had demonstrated how they might introduce the blood of a hound into the wound and bring forth something bestial in their gets, a creature that more closely resembled a dog, with a good many of the same physical attributes.

They set the dogs loose to prowl the grounds of the plantation and keep any of the Maroons foolish enough to consider stealing into the place at night at bay. Their predatory presence was enough to keep unruly slaves in line, too, shepherding them into their huts, where they couldn't cause mischief.

The grim truth of their slavery was that the Others didn't care if the dogs killed any of them, Maroons, or runaway slaves. It was never about control. It was about fear. It was about sending a message, and that message was: You can't escape. You can't win. This is your life now.

But that didn't stop the Maroons from coming or slaves from trying make a break for freedom. In truth, they had nowhere to run to, and the Others knew that. Human life was cheap, and, if the blood supply was depleted, it could be replenished easily enough.

What made the dogs special was their ability to move about at both dawn and dusk. Their tolerance to daylight was better than the Others, even if it was not absolute. It had been enough to give the Mistress the first glimmerings of an idea as to how she might just change everything: introduce human blood to one of the Others. It sounded naive, considering they needed human blood to thrive, but she was thinking beyond that, to a unique flavor of blood.

That was where the Queen of the Maroons came in. The source of her magic was the key; even a single drop of her blood mixed with that of other humans could well be the catalyst she needed to induce the transformation.

Of course, as potent as the bitch's magical blood was, it was highly unlikely any transformative effect would last more than minutes, or at best hours. It wouldn't be permanent because, like any nourishment blood offered the Others, it was in their nature to consume it. So the infusions would need to be repeated, over and over, whenever they sought to venture out of the darkness.

That would be the best of both worlds. It would give the Others what they so desperately craved—freedom—but would leave her indispensable. They would need her more than ever.

She poured herself another drink and leaned back into the wingback chair beside the guttering fire. Her host had left her alone, unable to resist the delights of the young slave girl they were tormenting. They had brought a few in for their pleasure. Let them play, she thought, glad of the peace it afforded her.

This was not their normal gathering. Most of the attendees were of mortal blood, but not all. There were several of the Others amongst them. It had been a chance to learn more in unguarded conversation about what the Others wanted.

Her hosts had been only too happy to lavish some of the finest foods their kitchen could produce and the best of their wine cellar, though they had drunk considerably more of it than she had during the meal. The alcohol had served its purpose and loosened their tongues. She had learned more in those few minutes than in weeks of eavesdropping and, at last, had begun to grasp the extent of their ambition.

She'd been mistaken in her belief that their desire to live part of their lives in daylight was motivated by a need for safety, although that was definitely part of it. Yes, there was increased safety in subduing enemies through dominance and control, bringing them to heel, but this went beyond even spreading their infection through the blood of other plantation owners. This was about building their empire.

As the wine had disappeared down their gullets, their tongues had grown looser, and it had become clear that their ambitions were even larger than just the island.

"And what is your price for helping us achieve this?" the Other had asked her, his words growing slurred even as a lascivious grin spread wide across his face.

Her answer came to her lips without thought. She could have demanded almost anything, and they would likely have promised it to her in that moment, so great was his appetite for what she was offering.

"Rose Hall," she said.

"Rose Hall?" He laughed at the absurdity of it. "The ruin of a building up on the hill? With the views out over the bay? Why?"

"I have my reasons," she said, without elaborating. He had no need to know her relationship to the place, or what was special about the land it stood upon.

"And that's all? You could have anything. You could have immortality, and that is all your little human heart desires?"

He was right. Of course he was. She could have asked for the world, and he would have promised it to her, without hesitation.

But greed led to ruin.

The house and the plantation, sitting on hundreds of acres of land that came with it, would be enough to ensure her comfort for the rest of her life, and she did not need them to help her extend it. She had her own gifts. Besides, forever was a very long time, and she had yet to find an immortal who truly considered the concept of eternity to mean exactly that.

"The man who owns it... you can leave him untouched. Believe me, I will be able to control him."

"So you intend to install yourself as the lady of the manor with the lord already in place?" The Other laughed delightedly, relishing the prospect. After all, why wouldn't he? He had seen her make the meat puppets dance for his pleasure and knew exactly what kind of control she could exert over the weak flesh. "Very well. I cannot imagine any of my kin will voice an objection. It shall be so."

It was only moments after that conversation that he excused himself, leaving her to the warmth of the fire and her thoughts of how she might lure the Queen of the Maroons out of her woodland hidey-hole to bleed. The copper vats used to collect the exsanguinated blood from feral strays to breed the Others' slave dogs were already in place in the cellar. They would be large enough for her needs. Now she just needed an irresistible bait to dangle from her trap.

The weakness all good people shared was their predictability. They could not abide the suffering of innocents or the torment of loved ones.

The Mistress expected her hosts to return from their entertainments before too long, and when they did, she could use them set her plan into motion.

SEVENTEEN

Saturday evening.

They were in place before the sun set. Each of them with at least three spears, blessed by Queen Nanny. She had weaved wardings around them, touching each with the magic of this place.

They had brought their bundles of firewood with them, laying them down beside hedges where they would not draw attention. It was one of the few benefits of the enemy's hubris: as long as they thought they were invincible, they would be careless.

It would be a while before the first of the carriages began to arrive. If they were lucky, they had a long night ahead of them.

If they weren't...

They hunkered down in the shadows, each silent as they waited. And waited. The tension was palpable. No one wanted to speak for fear of shattering whatever spell had fallen over them, keeping them safe from prying eyes. But there was no hiding from magic.

The first indication that the carriages had started to arrive was the distant clatter of hooves on the dry track and the rattle of steel-rimmed wheels.

Kwasi didn't dare breathe. He gripped the spears tight.

The full, bright moon flooded the landscape with its light, transforming leaf and branch to silver, the river's fast-running water to quicksilver and the silhouette of the carriages to a rifle shot rushing through the night.

They watched them all arrive, one by one, their cloaked and hooded drivers lashing the horses to drive them on, their passengers shrouded in the darkness within. It was only when they were sure that the last of the carriages had arrived that they dared move.

Queen Nanny slipped away, moving almost

silently as she followed the tree line. The backdrop of branches still swaying in the breeze reduced the risk of her movement drawing the eye. She made her way down to the gateway to the property, moving quickly but without rushing. If Kwasi hadn't known she was there, he would never have seen her, even as he followed close behind.

He carried a single spear, having left the others with Lima. Speed was more important than weapons; if they were discovered too soon, there would be no hope of the others completing their tasks.

He watched as she knelt beside the gatepost and heard her muttered incantation—the same words he had heard several times now—raising another of her defences. The difference, this time, was that the warding wasn't intended to keep the enemy out. It was meant to keep them inside. That was the crux of it; the only way they succeeded this night was if Queen Nanny's followers destroyed all of them.

Every last one.

A single enemy who escaped damned them all, and these things were like cockroaches... hard to kill.

He didn't believe they could end them all in a single night, but he had to act as if he did because his confidence fed into the others. They had increasingly begun looking to him as a warrior during his time with them. In his heart, though, he knew the best they could truly hope for was to thin their numbers and force them back to their nests.

There was one person inside who couldn't be allowed to escape, no matter what: the White Witch. With her control over the dead and her dark magics and twisted soul, she more than any of the blood-drinkers alone posed the greatest threat to their immediate survival. Her magic could strip them of the only defense they had—daylight.

And while there were many reasons the White Witch had to die, that was more than reason enough.

When Queen Nanny completed weaving her charm on the gateway, she rose to her feet and nodded to him. Kwasi drew the gate closed and wrapped a chain around the iron and the stone gatepost. The chains were fashioned from the same shackles some of them had worn as they had escaped their slave masters. There was a symmetry to using them to restrain the enemy now.

They made their way back to the others in silence. Several times along the way, Queen Nanny checked the sky or cast a glance toward the big house.

The time of reckoning drew ever closer. If they failed, the chains gave them a second chance with dawn coming to their aid, but they couldn't rely upon that.

More Maroons arrived. They began to drag

logs out of the undergrowth, hauling them over to the other side of the driveway. It was a simple snare, but ought to be enough to ensure the carriages were unable to turn easily, making retreat to the house all the more difficult. Everything was intended to hinder them, slow them down, rather than provoke direct and deadly confrontation. It didn't matter how seemingly trivial each inconvenience seemed on its own. Together, they became potentially lifesaving.

Or ending, depending upon your perspective.

This death by a thousand cuts wasn't Queen Nanny's only plan. She had another that she'd intended to fulfill on her own, but Kwasi had convinced her otherwise.

"You need someone to watch your back, Queen Nanny. I have seen you when you speak your incantations. It's as though you fall into a trance, oblivious to anything going on around you. That leaves you vulnerable. Any enemy could sneak up on you without you ever knowing."

"And you are offering to risk your own life to protect me?"

"I will do what it takes to keep you safe long enough to do what you must. If I lose my life in the process, so be it. As long as it buys you the time you need to save the others, it is a price worth paying," he had said.

She had nodded, content to accept his offer, even with its suicidal undertone.

While others moved more logs and branches and secured the gate, Kwasi followed Queen Nanny as she made her way farther from the house, cutting through the plantation fields until she reached the far side of the property that contained a fallow field, untended and unplanted.

Kwasi knew what this place was. It wasn't fallow at all. It was a graveyard where dead slaves were buried in unmarked graves and left to rot.

He had lost count of the number of men and women who had died on the plantation in the time he had labored there and could only imagine the true number buried in this place.

Why come here?

Queen Nanny offered no explanations. She crouched down, burying her hands in the dirt, and began to weave a fresh incantation, her voice rising and falling, falling and rising, with hypnotic intensity. Her voice weakened the longer she intoned those sounds he couldn't understand as actual words. Minutes became hours and hours multiplied, but she showed no sign of ending her incantation, even though nothing seemed to be happening.

Kwasi was ever vigilant, scanning the countryside for any sign of movement, from the fields all the way back to the main house and out across the trees, looking everywhere, determined to fulfill his promise. All he could do was watch and wait on edge the entire time.

At one point, he noticed a couple of figures had moved closer to them, darting close to the building and back again. Following their movements, he knew they were Maroons carrying out Queen Nanny's instructions.

His attention drifted up to the moon. They were running out of time.

Queen Nanny's voice shifted again, barely vocalizing the words now.

He saw the first of the carriages being brought back around to the front of the house. The enemy's evening of entertainment was coming to an end. In time more than thirty would leave this damned place.

They didn't have long. So many parts of Queen Nanny's plan had been put into place, but with time against them, he couldn't help but fear the enemy might still slip through their fingers, the opportunity lost.

Kwasi thought about rousing her from her incantations—it was obvious whatever she'd intended to do here was failing, and they needed her elsewhere if all wasn't to be lost.

He whispered her name, but she didn't respond.

"Queen Nanny?" he asked again urgently.

But the woman didn't falter, the music of her incantation weaving ever more delicately around him. He knew the sounds now, though they had lost all sense of separation over the hours he'd been listening to them. She was lost in the trance, swept up in the same repetitions.

He tried again, louder this time, but she was oblivious to his voice, even after he crouched down beside her, reaching out to shake her shoulder.

He couldn't draw her out of the trance. He was going to have to warn the others himself.

He started to stand, intending to run back to the gate, when he heard an unfamiliar noise, a scratching and scrambling in the undergrowth.

EIGHTEEN

For a moment, Kwasi thought he heard rats
scrambling through the tangled weeds all around
him, but then he heard voices approaching.
He crouched down for a moment as the voices
approached.

He was sure that he recognized one of them.
He'd heard it a thousand times and knew it better
than he knew his own. It was one of the overseers.
The one who had turned the whip on him during
his last days as a slave. The bastard never cared
whether it was a man, woman, or child that he
struck. He treated them all like animals.

Eventually, two men came into sight, one
carrying a bullwhip that he kept flicking out
in front of him, the other a cutlass, its blade
glinting now and then when it caught the
moonlight.

Kwasi had his spear and his knife. They had to

be enough.

They were deep in trivial conversation, not looking for anyone. That was good. It meant he had a chance. Nothing suggested they were the enemy's changelings fresh from the party, either. They were mortal men, and mortal men could surely die.

They were making their rounds, a cursory check of the plantation to ensure the slaves were in their place. That gave Kwasi hope. He had the element of surprise, and if he struck fast, that more than evened out the odds.

He tensed, prepared to spring.

And in that moment, he realized he had delayed a moment too long.

The men spied him and Queen Nanny, stopping them in their tracks. He expected them to call out a challenge, but they didn't.

Rather, they seemed more disturbed by the sounds of scratching all around them than the sight of Queen Nanny and him. The man with the whip flicked it through the undergrowth, the crack loud in the still night. He couldn't see anything in there. And yet the noise grew ever louder and more insistent.

Kwasi felt the earth rumble beneath his feet. A lurch of movement accompanied the rising sound, and then suddenly, he heard the rush of dirt shifting, spilling, something breaking up through the soil.

All around him, the ground shivered. Something was breaking free. Clumps of rough grass and sod ripped, rising and parting as they were forced aside.

It wasn't rats.

In moments, there were dozens of patches of bare soil being disturbed, something beneath pushing up against the dirt until it broke free from each of them.

It took him a moment to realize what he was seeing, even as they caught the moonlight, silver rather than ivory.

Hands!

They clawed at the air, scrabbled at the earth, scraping it away.

The two overseers backed away. It took a moment for the reality of what was happening all around them to sink in—but they had seen enough weirdness to know they were not imagining the horrors of the slaves' graveyard. These hands clawing their way out of the ground were coming for them. Surrounding them.

The two men scrambled about in a frenzied dance, trying to find sound footing as more and more of the ground kept betraying them. More hands clawed their way upward, each in different stages of decay. Some of the more recently buried were still fresh, with worms and caked with earth, while others were so rotten it was obvious that they'd been in the ground months if not years, and others still were barely more than bones.

The two men tried to find a pathway among the grasping dead hands as they clawed at their ankles.

In front of them, one of the dead emerged from what should have been its final resting place, its head pushing out through the film of mud in a parody of rebirth.

The slaver with the cutlass hacked and slashed at the thing, sliced wildly through arms that fell to the ground. The loss wasn't enough to stop its owner from rising to its knees, then unsteadily to its feet and stumbling toward him.

Kwasi seized the moment, snatching up his spear. He hurled the blessed weapon at the slaver with the bullwhip, determined not to have his vengeance stolen from him.

The spear found its mark, plunging deep into the man. He cried out in pain and surprise, clutching at the wooden shaft as he fell to the ground.

The other man stood his ground. And in moments, he was overwhelmed by the risen dead and dragged to the ground, smothered by the crush of decay.

The man gave a final cry, then fell silent.

And still the growing mass of resurrected corpses continued to rise, trampling over the fallen bodies.

For a sickening moment, Kwasi stood rooted to the earth, recognizing the face of an old friend riddled with worms as he clawed his way out of the ground.

Sickness churned in his gut.

He couldn't keep looking.

He needed to move. Be gone. Away from this place.

Kwasi snatched up the cutlass and looked at the faces of the dead as they shuffled past him. He recognized more than he cared to admit, even if the grave had changed their features and they wore the earth like death masks.

There were at least a hundred of them, perhaps even twice that many. They were on the move, in search of their own revenge.

Bodies stumbled past Kwasi, brushing against him, close enough for him to smell their decay. Instead of gagging against the corruption, the odor that filled the air was the smell of hope.

Queen Nanny was on her feet now, fully aware that the dead were dancing to her tune.

THE OLD WORLD:
A FORGOTTEN TIME,
A FORGOTTEN PLACE
III

Nanny sat in silence.

She watched the elder woman labor over
preparations, carefully mixing herbal unctions
and salves that might be used to heal minor
wounds. It was a skill, even if it lacked the thrill
of the earth magic. She had been summoned to
learn. It was a part of who they were, she had
said, and that the ancient knowledge must pass
through the bloodlines, though with no daughter
of her own, the elder woman was afraid that
everything she had learned, the collective wisdom
of their tribe's wise women, would be lost. So
she had taken Nanny under her wing, sharing
little parcels of the old ways. She had summoned
Nanny tonight because she had something

important to tell her, something that might one day save her life.

Nanny had been given no other hint to what she might be about to witness, but she would never dare question the elder woman. So she waited in silence, watching the painstaking labors and precise measures as her guardian made her concoctions. She would be told eventually. There would be time for questions after. But there was never any promise of answers. Some things she was expected to work through for herself. Knowledge learned was more valuable than wisdom simply handed down, as the elder woman often told her. Which had an ironic ring to it, given what they were doing together.

"Time to go," the elder woman said, snatching up her bag.

Nanny nodded and stood.

It wasn't unusual for them to leave the village under cover of darkness, but this was different. The elder woman had been uncommonly quiet for a while now, weighed down with concern over what might be about to happen. Nanny had felt it. This was a moment of importance.

They left behind the little hut she had called home for so long. The world was wrapped up in silence. Candles burned in a few of the other dwellings they saw as they walked. She heard a few hushed voices. It was normal. Lovers' midnight whispers. Promises shared, bodies enjoyed. It was life. But Nanny knew otherwise. There was nothing normal about the dangers out there, beyond the shadows that marked the circumference of the village. She had seen those dangers closer than she could ever have wanted to.

There was no telling how far they walked. The darkness made it impossible to keep track of time, and while there were plenty of nocturnal forest sounds, animals out there on the hunt, she didn't feel afraid. Had she been alone, though, it would have been different.

Without warning, the elder woman stopped. "This is the place," she said.

Nanny looked around, trying to see anything that made the place special, but there was nothing to see. It was a clearing, just like dozens upon dozens of clearings they had walked through already. Moonlight lit the ground in the center of the space, but there were darkness and shadows all around them.

"Where are we?" Nanny asked.

"This is a sacred grove. It is where we bury our dead," the elder woman replied.

Nanny couldn't remember the last time any of their number had died. There had been a man, a tall, friendly man whose name slipped just beyond the reach of memory. He had been taken by the beasts one night, and there had been so little of him left when they had finished with him that he had been taken somewhere without ceremony. It was the last burial she knew of. She hadn't been present, as she had been a child.

There had been others, but again, she did not recall the details beyond the vaguest memories—he had been bitten, and they had been forced to kill him before he had killed them. But he hadn't been buried. The elder woman had insisted on destroying his body with fire, a fire that she had conjured up herself. Nanny was sure that she'd never been to this place before.

"Sit," her guardian insisted, pointing toward a fallen log. "You must watch every move I make, listen to every sound that escapes my lips, and commit them to memory. The time will come, one day far from this place, when your life and the life of others will depend on your memory of this night. Fail, and everyone close to you will perish. I have seen it.

"This is a rite unlike any other that takes you to dangerous places of the soul and should only ever be practiced in the direst of moments when all hope has failed. Understand?"

She nodded.

"Good. Now listen."

Nanny had seen the woman work with tallow candles in other rituals, not that she needed the light, but because the flame gave her something to concentrate on; a single, fixed point when the world seemed to shift around her. Not this time. There was no comforting flame, only the light of the moon.

The elder woman took her time, removing various items from her sackcloth bag and setting them down on the ground in front of her. Nanny had seen some of them before: various leather pouches of healing herbs, a splinter of wood she would set to smoldering that burned with a heady aroma, among other things. But she had never seen the bone before.

She found her mind taken back to the night of the attack—that fateful night when families had been torn apart and loved ones taken, including her own mother. She remembered the bones protruding from damaged flesh. How could she forget?

And then the chanting began.

The end of the stick had been set alight, the elder woman whispering one of her tricks to bring the flame to life long enough to stir a heat within the wood before the flames were extinguished. A trail of smoke rose from it. She pushed the other end of the splinter into the earth, keeping it upright.

The incantation continued, the words spinning around and around them, this time with hands upraised, then lowered again. But the more intently she listened, the harder it became to focus on the words themselves. They were barely audible.

Nanny picked up a few words, but not many, that had no real meaning, until suddenly she understood. It was as if something had tripped inside her mind and she could comprehend, whole lines becoming both coherent and potent.

She found her own lips moving in time with

the elder woman's, mimicking the words as best she could as they seared into her memory while she raised and lowered her own hands in tandem with her guardian. Hers was an instinctive education.

The true potency of the incantation began to slowly make itself known to her as the chanting went on for an hour, and then another, without any immediately obvious effect. Neither woman ceased their chant, the words building in intensity and passion as the command became irresistible and the ground cracked.

It was little more than a jagged line in the dust to begin with, but they demanded more, and slowly, it grew in length and widened in answer.

Something started moving down there.

In that moment, fear gripped Nanny, and she could no longer maintain her shadowing of the conjuration. She managed to stop herself from scrambling back in panic as something began to claw its way up out of the ground. She sat there, slack-jawed and dumbstruck.

A fist caked in dirt pushed its way clear of the ground. Flakes of dried clay clung to it, then crumbled away as the hand stretched, the fist opening wide, and then began scratching and scrambling to reach the open air.

It was a sight that defied reason. But the fear was replaced by fascination and a sudden urge to help whoever it was that had been buried alive. She needed to get them out of the ground before the dirt clogged their lungs and they suffocated.

It didn't cross her mind that the thing trying to free itself was already dead until a strip of flesh fell away with the dirt to reveal bone beneath.

And even then, she did not feel afraid. She recovered her senses, understanding the true extent of the elder woman's power and how death held no dominion here. She had brought life to something long buried and longer dead.

"You understand now, girl?"

Nanny nodded. She understood. Of all the conjurations she had ever witnessed, this was by far the most powerful, defying death itself.

Her lips rejoined the chant once again.

NINETEEN

Kwasi couldn't keep count of how many of them there were. Easily double the number of the living who had come with him and Queen Nanny to the plantation. More. And they acted under the direction of Queen Nanny like she was some powerful puppeteer.

He struggled with what he had seen, but he had the evidence of his own eyes.

The dead had risen from their graves. It had all been her doing.

And now she led them as a mob through the sugar cane, trampling on anything that lay in their way. It was her army, created with no fear of death or of what the enemy could do to them because they were already well beyond their reach.

When they began to walk, Kwasi had expected them to shuffle toward the plantation house, drawn to the enemy, but that wasn't what happened. Queen Nanny sent them to the driveway and the barred gate where the Maroons manned the barricades, ready to fight for their lives when the enemy tried to leave this place.

As they crested the rise and saw the lane reaching out, Kwasi realized there was already a small queue of coaches waiting to pass through the gate that was going nowhere.

Queen Nanny raised a hand and uttered a single word.

It meant nothing to Kwasi, but it obviously did to the dead, because the moment she lowered her hand, the horde picked up speed and moved as one toward the coaches.

Their unsteady gait ate up the ground, despite their varying level of decay, with the bodies forming a single mob that moved with a single mind. Queen Nanny matched them stride for stride.

Kwasi had no desire to be left behind, but

keeping up with them as they plowed on through the churned earth was exhausting, and he very quickly found keeping up with them difficult.

As they drew closer to the driveway, a cluster of dead men peeled off from the stumbling mob, turning their attention to the last carriage as it left the house.

Kwasi did his very best to keep them in sight so that he could see what they were doing. Should he stay with Queen Nanny, or would he serve better by aiding this smaller group in their fight against the enemy?

He needn't have concerned himself. They did not need him. A moment later, a piercing scream tore from the horses' mouths as they bucked and reared in their harnesses, fighting to be free of them to flee. Their cries were pure panic, but changed the longer they sounded, until all he could hear inside them was pain.

Even in the moonlight, Kwasi saw that they had been set upon, and the dead were tearing at their flesh with savage hunger. The poor animals didn't stand a chance.

How long they had lain in the ground?

How long had it been since they had last fed?

How desperate were those appetites to be sated?

Whatever the answer to those questions, the dead didn't care what flesh they consumed, only that they gorged themselves. They were as ruthless as any of the enemy's pets, and what they might have lacked in physical strength, they more than made up for in numbers, overwhelming the horses, dragging them down, and tearing into them in a tooth-and-bony-clawed frenzy.

The horses bucked and reared and screeched, iron-shod hooves hammering down, but the carriage toppled with the dead swarming over it.

It fell with a crash, the strain tearing the frame apart, freeing the still-tethered horses. No longer bound to the carriage, the lucky few bolted with the undead clinging to them as they made their escape, even as the others lost their lives to the mob.

A shocking crack and deep rending of wood under the weight of the horde rang out. Then one of the doors was flung free.

It was impossible to see what was going on within the toppled carriage, but Kwasi knew whoever was inside would fight like a feral cat, desperate not to be restrained even as more and more of the dead swarmed over them. Could the dead destroy the enemy? Would their teeth and bony fingers gouge deep enough to rip out the enemy's hearts? Would that even stop them? Could they destroy those denizens of the night?

It was hard to imagine anyone, or anything, being able to stand up to their attack. They were rabid, the dead.

Kwasi turned his attention to the carriages trying to force a way out through the gateway, but the chains held.

The Maroons manning the barricade hurled

their blessed spears at the carriages. Some, he saw, blazed through the sky, and he realized they had been set alight.

The fire alone was enough to frighten the horses. The driver of one of the carriages tried to turn around, but his wagon became jammed up against the logs that had been laid against the side of the track. Still, the horses pulled, desperate to obey their master's bidding. The strain was enough to wrench one of the wheels from its axle. A burning spear thunked into another of the coaches, and within the space of two heartbeats, its fire engulfed it. The spread of the flames was unnaturally fast. Kwasi knew that that had to be Queen Nanny's doing. He saw her standing alone, intently watching everything unfold around her.

A flurry of movement drew his eye: a black shape slipping away from one of the coaches.

His breath caught in his throat. It had to be one of the enemy.

Queen Nanny had seen it, too. She loosened a call, and her army of the dead stopped in their tracks, dropping whatever they had in their hands, be it horse meat or spurs of broken carriage wood, and turned on the shadow-shape. And still it almost succeeded in evading them.

Almost, but not quite.

It ran fast, a darker blur against the black of the forest, but the horde were faster. They fell upon it, dragging it down, and it was lost beneath the mass of the dead and decaying.

There were screams. This time, it wasn't the sound of the horses.

But it wasn't the enemy or their servants, either, even as they were swept up in the melee. It was something else.

Kwasi glanced to Queen Nanny. He saw the exhaustion on her face. The screams, whatever made them, were not her doing.

Move movement, more screams.

He saw silhouettes spilling out of the manor

house, moving preternaturally fast. The enemy's pets. It took Kwasi a moment to realize that they didn't remain silhouettes for long and that he could see them clearly, when only a few moments ago, they would have still been shrouded in darkness as they emerged.

The world was changing around him, and it wasn't just the backwash of light from the flames consuming the carriages. The sky had grown lighter. Dawn was close. Only a few moments away. And when it broke, those things would be trapped outside in the daylight, with no safe place to hide before the light hunted them down.

The pets turned, bounding back toward the house, but there was something disturbingly wrong with the way they moved.

Moments later, they were howling, the inhuman screams torn from their snouts becoming infinitely more human as smoke wisped from their fur. As desperately as they tried to run, they couldn't save themselves. It was too late for them, too late for any of the enemy and their minions who were stranded far from the safety of the house.

The dead stumbled back from the carriages, their work done.

In an instant, the ruined carriages were engulfed in flames. Raucous cheers rose from the Maroons still standing behind the barricades, the last of their spears still clutched in their hands, ready to fight anything that tried to escape.
No one, and no thing, was getting through the gateway they defended.

They had done everything they had set out to do, and more, and they had won a massive victory against the enemy, though the fight was far from over.

But for now, this was a moment to be savored. They had severely depleted the ranks of the enemy.

The dead stood away from the burning carriages, not approaching the Maroons. To

Kwasi, they seemed lost, unsure of what they were supposed to do next.

TWENTY

Kwasi knew more of the Enemy were in the
house. Their work was not done. The place had to
be destroyed, as did every last one of the damned
creatures that had turned it into their nest.

Nanny set off marching across the dirt
toward the big house and the remains of the
wretched creatures that had been transformed
to do the enemy's bidding. They lay charred and
smoldering on the grass, posing her no threat.

She carried the sword again, but now it
appeared like a burden to her, a weight she
struggled to bear. Whereas not so very long ago
she had run across the cane fields with no effort
at all, outpacing him and outlasting him, now it
took a colossal effort for the woman to simply
put one foot in front of the other.

"Let me," he said, hurrying to catch up with
her. He reached out a hand, offering, "Let me

carry the blade for you."

He didn't ask why they were going to the house while the others were leaving. He trusted her implicitly.

Of all of them, Queen Nanny understood the enemy they faced. She knew what needed to be done. He could not allow her to face this fight alone. Not while there was a breath in his body— or, given the nature of their allies in this fight, long after the last one had been drawn.

She handed the weapon over, her body seeming to slump as relief flooded her system. There was no reluctance. He was glad to take the burden.

"We must hurry," she said. "Find them in their nests before their human servants can protect them from us, and we must end them where they lie. There won't be any second chances. This is the night, and this one alone. They will not make the same mistake twice. But those servants are every bit as human as you or I. Under the enemy's spell or not, they are not affected by day or night."

"How can we tell if the living in there have been bent to the enemy's will or if they have been coerced to work for them... I mean, how can we judge innocence from guilt and who needs to die in there?"

"We give them the opportunity to run," she said. "Only an innocent soul will take it. We may even find one. But heed this: the enemy would never risk betrayal. Anyone who walks freely inside that place does so because they have the enemy's trust. There are no innocents in there. If you tell someone to run and they do not, you cannot hesitate for even a second. They will not show you mercy. Believe me."

The dead were moving again. Kwasi felt as much as heard the movement coming from behind them.

He glanced back to see them gathering themselves together, clustering up until they formed a single mass again and begin to shuffle closer. There was no blind charge this time. It was cautious, careful, with them following Queen Nanny.

The front door of the house hung open, inviting them in.

Kwasi and Queen Nanny lingered for a moment on the threshold. He offered her the sword.

She shook her head. "Keep it," she said as she took a step inside. "May it serve you well if you are called upon to use it."

He nodded his understanding and set his scavenged spear aside—it was no match for the weapon he held now—leaning it against the doorframe before following her inside.

The house was filled with a jaundiced light from outside. There was no sign of anyone, neither agent of the enemy nor their servants. The pair of them looked left and right, listening for a sound, for anything that might lead them one way over another in their search. The layout of this part of the house seemed similar to the plantation house Kwasi had been inside when they'd taken Afua. He found himself remembering crouching on the stone steps leading down to the underground space where they'd tethered and caged their pets. It placed a chill in his heart, but even as it did, he knew.

"The cellars," he said, knowing it had to be the truth.

Queen Nanny led the way. She didn't wait to see if he followed. She swung open one door after another along a corridor until she found the one she was looking for. It revealed a dark stairwell rather than leading into a room. The stairs themselves were in near darkness, with an oil lamp fixed to the wall at the bottom, creating a puddle of light just large enough to reveal another door.

"Follow me down," Queen Nanny said, not giving him the chance to be chivalrous.

The air behind him blossomed with the scent of damp earth and decay. It was enough to send him hurrying down the wooden steps after her. He cast a backward glance up toward the light and saw the crush of the dead remained at the doorway, not moving any closer. That, at least, was a relief of sorts. And no one would get past them, so Kwasi didn't need to worry about covering their backs.

He still took each stair down with care, not wanting to make so much as a creak of sound for fear of what would stir.

He reached the bottom. The space was barely large enough for the two of them to stand, but he waited while Queen Nanny murmured more words he could not follow, her hands pressed against the wood of the door.

When she finally stopped with her low-pitched chant and stepped back, he moved past her and swung the door open, sword at the ready.

He was not sure what he'd expected to find

on the other side—maybe some sort of pen with shackles chained to the stone walls where their pets were kept during the day, living in their own filth. There was nothing like that. Rather, it resembled an industrial arrangement with great copper vats in the center of a much larger room. Above one of the vats hung a naked man, strung up by his ankles, his wrists and throat both cut, the blood that had spilled staining his black skin. That blood dripped slowly from the body, a steady drip echoing around the room.

It was the only sound, louder than Kwasi's heartbeat in his ears. Otherwise, there was silence.

How long had that poor bastard's lifeblood been leaking into the vat? Days? Weeks? What sort of sick torture was this?

He felt his anger rising uncontrollably. Frustration burned inside him. His fist clenched around the sword's hilt. He wanted nothing more than for one of the enemy to wake and come blundering into the room so that he had something to take his anger out on. The poor man hanging from the ceiling deserved justice.

But his rage was nothing compared with that of Queen Nanny. She screamed with fury, the sound still filling the room when her army of the dead surged down the stairs and through the doorway.

She did not need to tell them what to do. Her emotion alone was enough.

The dead knew. Together, they pushed against the great copper vats, the pipework squealing and straining under the pressure until they started to move, tearing out of the walls.

It seemed to take forever, but the dead rocked the largest of the vats backward and forward in its support, the blood within sloshing with each motion, until it spilled over the sides, drenching the animated corpses, and the dead found the strength to topple the huge vat.

So much blood spilled into the room, taking

down pipets and other equipment smashing to the floor, as the dead went to topple the second vat.

The blood seemed to send them into a frenzy, but it wasn't mindless. Everything they did was controlled, concerted, the mind behind it Queen Nanny's.

Kwasi found something to stand on, reaching up to support the dangling corpse with one arm and hack at the rope with the other. It took several slices with the blade before it sheered through and the body was free.

The weight was too much for him to bear, but he did his best to lower it to the ground with dignity, even though he laid it in its own blood and that of who knew how many others. It seemed a terrible thing to do to it, but it felt like less of an abomination than leaving the victim hanging from the ceiling.

He stood up from his crouch, his sword arm loose at his side, blood staining his clothes and skin, and the blade in his hand. He looked like furious vengeance made flesh. And in that moment, that was exactly what he had become.

"We have to find them," Queen Nanny said. The urgency in her voice was unmistakeable.

THE OLD WORLD: A FORGOTTEN TIME, A FORGOTTEN PLACE

IV

"How did you know you had the gift? Was it always there in you?" Nanny asked, not for the first time. "Or were you taught, like you've taught me?"

Previously, the elder woman had always waved the question away as if it was of no importance. But something had changed in her demeanor this time. Perhaps it was because she was getting frail as time ate away at her day by day. She barely left the shelter of their small hut other than to ensure that their small village was safe from the enemy. And some nights now, she wasn't well enough to do that and was forced to rely on Nanny to carry out even the simplest tasks.

It wasn't about trust or having passed some

test to prove her strength. With the sun high in the sky, her guardian still had not left her bed. In all their days together, Nanny had never known her to have a moment of illness before. The decline was painful to see.

"Ah girl, of course others showed me how to do the things I can do. I did not conjure the magic from thin air." Her smile was gentle. "A good woman, far wiser than me, showed me how to mix my herbs and drilled into me the words to make the invocations work. But you are right to think there is more to some of the things I can do than simply practice and more power behind it that any mere ritual. That is the power of the land itself... but... it is never as simple as just that."

Nanny waited, saying nothing. The elder woman tried to continue but was struggling to catch her breath.

Nanny handed her a clay flask of water and held it to her lips while the elder woman drank a little before slumping back on her bed. Even this bit of exertion exhausted her.

"There is something that helps me," she said, finding her voice again, though now it was barely above a whisper. "A gift I was given when I was little older than you. You have done me proud, girl, achieving more than I dared dream when I first found you... You can control many of the magics I have shown you, but there are some that may be beyond you without a similar gift. Do you understand?"

"The dead man," Nanny said, thinking that she did. "The thing you did with him?"

The elder woman nodded. "I think I forgot just how much I have relied upon that gift over the years, but now that this body is wearing out, it's time for me to pass it on to you."

"Please, don't talk that way. We have time."

The elder woman gave out something like a laugh, though it turned into a fit of coughing. When it subsided, there was still a rattle in her chest, and to Nanny, it seemed as if she had aged in even those few moments. Was it truly possible her life was almost over? Nanny tried to hold back the tears, but it was far from easy to deny them.

The elder woman was still talking, or at least, her lips were still moving, but Nanny couldn't make out what she was saying. She moved closer until she felt her ragged breath on her face.

The elder woman raised a hand to Nanny's cheek, the dry, leathery skin pressing against her own, but then she reached around the back of Nanny's head, preventing her from pulling away.

Nanny panicked for a moment, unsure of what was happening and not liking the feel of it.

The elder woman opened her mouth wider, her breath impossibly hot. Feverish. Nanny struggled frantically to pull away, but the grip was vicelike.

"Please," Nanny whimpered, and still the woman did not release her.

"It is a gift," she said. "Do not be afraid." She released a breath that was both hot and fetid.

Nanny tried not to breathe it in but couldn't help herself. That hot, sweet, sickly breath found its way, thick and tangible, into her. She coughed, trying to purge it from her body, then helplessly gulped down another mouthful of air and another, until the elder woman released her at last.

Gasping, she reeled back.

"What was that?" Nanny demanded, coughing and trying to expel from her lungs whatever she had breathed in.

The elder woman slumped back even deeper into her cot, seeming smaller somehow. There was almost nothing of her left. She seemed older, so much older, the skin on her face cracked and flaked as if her soul was in the process of shedding a skin it no longer needed.

"I told you... That was my gift," she said. "The last thing I can give you."

"But what was it?"

Nanny barely heard the last words to come from the elder woman's lips before life slipped away from her. And in the days to come, she would try to convince herself that she had misheard them, that they could not have been what she'd heard. But there was no denying the truth of them because she felt the thing inside her.

"A demon."

TWENTY-ONE

They went from door-to-door downstairs until they were done with the entire ground floor, without encountering another soul until they reached the kitchens, where a number of slaves clustered in fear. They bolted at the sight of Kwasi with the sword. Two didn't. Kwasi realized they were overseers, relaxing by the stove as they enjoyed the home comforts the plantation had on offer.

They leaped to their feet as Kwasi and Queen Nanny entered the kitchens, ready to take the fight to them until the first of the dead stumbled through.

The fear flared bright in their eyes. They wanted to run, that much was obvious, but something stopped them. A greater fear? What could be more terrifying than the sight of the dead stumbling toward them and the knowledge that their own death was the only possible way this confrontation would end?

One glanced toward the door the female slaves had fled through. Still, he didn't move.

Kwasi cut off the escape route. He had given the overseers the moment he'd promised Queen Nanny before judging them guilty. Their one chance gone, he stepped toward them, his blade swinging. Behind him, more of the dead shuffled forward.

Queen Nanny raised a hand to stop them. They were not needed at that moment.

It took a single swing to dispatch the first of the men. His head hit the floorboards a fraction of a second before his lifeless body.

For a moment, Kwasi thought it was going to be enough to break the hold the enemy had over the other man, but it wasn't. As his companion fell, he threw himself at Kwasi, snatching up a long, thin-bladed knife from one of the chopping surfaces and screaming with rage as he launched himself forward.

Kwasi's blade was already in position without him having to think about defense, skewering the overseer with his own momentum. Surprise flared across the other man's face, but beneath it, he was sure he saw relief. Free at last.

The man slumped to the floor, guts spilling out with his lifeblood, and sprawled beside his fallen comrade.

It was done.

Through the window, Kwasi saw the women were running away. None gave so much as a backward glance. Were they frightened of what they might see back there or more focused on the hope that lay beyond the slave huts and the forest where the Maroons made their home?

He would know soon enough if the women had chosen to swell their ranks or to die, assuming he made it out of this house alive.

The house was huge, a warren of corridors,

chambers, nooks, and crannies. But even so, it didn't take them long to finish searching the final few corners downstairs.

At the foot of the grand stair, Queen Nanny slumped, the exhaustion filling her face as she reached out for the balustrade to stop herself from falling.

Kwasi was at her side in a heartbeat, steadying her. "Are you alright?"

She nodded, drawing a deep breath. "But I can't hold them anymore. I have to let them go."

"Then let them go. They deserve their sleep," Kwasi said, understanding immediately.

She closed her eyes and lowered her head, a single word escaping her lips. Her entire body collapsed in on itself then, but rather than fall, she straightened as if she had a pain that was slowly subsiding.

The dead left them. They streamed through the open doorway, pushing after one another in the crush to reach the sun, leaving the detritus of their rotten bodies as they left.

The Maroons, inside the house, had to take this fight to the enemy now. It wasn't enough that they had destroyed their contraptions in the cellar. Blood could always be replaced. There were always slaves to bleed.

They needed to do more. They needed to find the nests where the enemy bedded down and purge them, taking their heads from their shoulders and cutting out their hearts. She barked out orders to her people. It fell to Kwasi and Nanny to find the White Witch and run the blade through her heart. Only then could they finish the cleansing by setting light to the entire place and watching it burn while the fire consumed the enemy's corpses and all of their pets and servants.

Nothing could remain.

Nothing.

Outside, the dead moved as one once more, their shuffling gait leading them back toward the field they had been summoned from. Only when the last of them had left did Kwasi look back at Queen Nanny.

She had shaken off his hand and stood now, revitalized and ready to carry on, her burden lightened. She led the way, marching up the stairs, Kwasi close behind.

Bedroom after bedroom lay unoccupied, though it was obvious the beds had been used recently. At last, they came to a chamber where they discovered a woman lying on the bed while an old man sat a lonely vigil in the chair beside her.

In an eerily sad manner, it was reminiscent of the scene they had stumbled across days ago when they'd found the enemy with the young woman. The man appeared frail and offered little threat. Looking at the pathetic wretch on the bed, the same could be said for the woman.

Kwasi took a step to back out of the room, but Queen Nanny stopped him.

"We are not done here," she said, touching his arm to prevent him from leaving. "Whatever you see, he is one of the enemy—one of the worst of them."

Kwasi looked at the man, who had not moved from his chair.

One hand had snaked out to hold the woman's hand, taking comfort from her touch.

She hadn't made a sound since Kwasi and Queen Nanny had entered the room. Her breathing was labored, each shallow exhalation like a death rattle.

"You are too late," the old man said.

"Too late? No," Queen Nanny said. "It doesn't matter to me how you die, only that you breathe your last."

"Foolish child. There has already been a sacrifice," he said, the pleasure in his voice unmistakable. "And it will guarantee the survival of my kind and the decline of your own. You have already lost this fight."

The old man grew progressively frailer by the moment as daylight stole in around the edges of the heavy drapes.

Kwasi had seen enough in another room just like this one to know the two were related. All he had to do was tear down the drapes, and this would be over. There was little to be gained by prolonging it. Killing the pair of them would be a mercy, but Queen Nanny wasn't in the business of mercy. She stood there, a dark angel, staring down at the enemy.

Kwasi made a step toward them. He thought the old man might to try to prevent him, but all he did was lean over the old woman and touch his mouth to her neck.

It was a tender moment. A last kiss before the light took them both.

A final goodbye.

But when he turned to look up Kwasi, his smile was smeared with blood.

There was a new vitality in his movements, an

energy that hadn't been there before. His smile split wider, exposing the too-long teeth Kwasi had seen before.

Kwasi raised his sword in readiness.

Faster than he had any right to be, the old man leaped toward Queen Nanny, gnarled and leathery hands reaching out, mouth snarling wide. The attack was viper fast; there was nothing Kwasi could do to stop him.

Queen Nanny stretched her arms out as if in supplication, as if to fend the fiend off, but there was no way she would be able to hold him back.

Kwasi's world came down to three people: the old woman on the bed, blood at her throat, and the old man overcoming Queen Nanny while Kwasi stood there, helpless to save or damn anyone.

TWENTY-TWO

Queen Nanny grasped the danger of what was happing too late.

The woman on the bed was not one of the enemy, not in the truest sense of the word. She might have run with them, just as other animals might run with a pack for defense, even in knowledge that in doing so they risked the pack turning on them to feed.

But if she was not one of them, she must have something vital to offer in return for her life.

She was the one they called the White Witch.

Queen Nanny had imagined she would be younger, some upstart high on the power of the old ways, with no control and filled with the desire for power that was so seductive. She had never seen the woman in close quarters before. Even as she stared down at her, Queen Nanny saw that the deep-cut lines on her face and her pallid and cracked skin made her seem older than she really was.

She understood it all then, the trade the White Witch had made to become part of their cabal. She had offered the enemy what they needed most: her vitality.

It was then that Queen Nanny knew that the White Witch had discovered key to unlocking the enemy's true desire of walking abroad in daylight. The final piece of the puzzle fell into place as the old man bent over her and pierced her throat.

It wasn't the slave who had been hanging over the vat of blood who was the sacrifice that night.

It was her.

Queen Nanny.

And then the old man was turning toward Queen Nanny, his mouth smeared with blood, teeth stained red. Everything about the fiend was preternaturally fast, his movements too quick for her to do anything to fend him off. She barely managed to call out the first syllable of Kwasi's name, not that he could have move quickly enough to intercede. No, she could only hope that he had grasped the truth of the moment; there was only one way to stop the enemy.

She must be sacrificed.

The fiend was on her in an instant, his teeth at her throat, pressing against her flesh.

She felt those fangs puncture her skin. It was only then she released the scream she'd been struggling to set free.

A fraction too late, Kwasi lunged for the drapes, desperately trying to open them and let the daylight in. They were heavier than he'd expected, and thicker, with heavy backing to ensure the light didn't filter through. That made them reluctant to move, but he used all his strength to haul them crashing to the floorboards.

The sudden spear of light lancing into the bedchamber was enough to draw a cry of pure bloodcurdling agony from the enemy. He might have looked like an old man, but no wrinkles or desiccated skin could ever convey just how ancient the creature was. It pulled away from Queen Nanny, rounding on Kwasi.

The sunlight touched its skin, and as it crept from throat to forehead, it left a trail of dust in its wake. It took no time at all, the silence between heartbeats. Skin smoldering, it was no longer able to stand and was denied the voice to utter another cry despite the undeniable agony consuming its body. The ash stole into every deep-cut wrinkle, spreading across the planes of its cheeks and into the hollows of its eyes, working its way deeper and deeper until the enemy's skull collapsed in on itself and its body crumbled.

Kwasi managed a half step back. In that single moment, there was nothing but the creature's clothes left smoking on the ground.

He stepped through the debris to reach Queen Nanny. She had a trembling hand raised to her neck. It came away slick with blood.

Blood pounded through her skull. It drowned out everything in this world.

She felt sickness clawing deep within her gut and knew it was her body's natural revulsion from the enemy's tainted kiss.

She was in trouble here.

Anger laced with fear warred within her, threatening to overwhelm Queen Nanny, but she couldn't give in to it.

The only thing she could do was believe the gift she'd been given by the elder woman would yet be her salvation. And if it wasn't... Well, then, the alternative did not bear thinking about. She'd rather be dead, no longer part of this fight, than to become one of them. She looked toward the bed and the rumpled tangle of cotton sheets.

Too late, Queen Nanny heard footsteps rushing along the hallway, heavy steps belonging to people who didn't care if they were heard. Until that moment, the pounding in her ears had drowned everything else out.

Rough hands grabbed her and wrapped something around her. Whatever it was, the bite of it made her scream when it touched her skin.

Heavy iron chains bound her arms to her sides. All the strength went from her.

No longer able to support herself, Queen Nanny's legs gave way.

The metal chains were impossibly heavy, but it was more than the sheer weight that overcame her. Something inside her fell quiet, the iron silencing it.

She was cut off from the gift she had been given all those years ago.

It was no longer able to help her.

"Run!" Queen Nanny howled, but that word may have only existed inside her head.

She had no idea if Kwasi did as she ordered him or if he stayed to fight before the blackness overtook her.

IN THE LAIR OF
THE WHITE WITCH
III

The Mistress had not slept for two days and nights.

She had remained by the vats, murmuring her incantations as the blood slowly decanted from the last of the slaves taken from their huts and from others brought in from neighboring estates.

The Others had a vested interest in making sure she succeeded in her efforts, but even failure offered some pleasure if it meant the perpetual thorns in their sides, the Maroons, and their damned bitch of a leader were finally put down.

The corpses, drained of every drop of blood, had been hung from trees along the fringes of the woodland, traps baited. She knew through the Others that these tracks were well trodden by the Maroons. The bodies would be found. The message was being sent, and to a certain kind of person, it would be irresistible.

Let them come, she thought.

They would imagine they were striking at the heart of the enemy, without ever understanding they were doing her bidding every bit as much as if she was in their meat puppets making them dance.

The Others had gathered that night, with heated discussions revolving around the threat they faced and the constant, thorny irritation the Maroons and their unnatural queen were. With threats and boasts shared, talk swiftly moved on to fantasy, with them describing with great relish how they would eliminate her once and for all before they set about enjoying the pleasures of the flesh, their lusts inflamed.

They had been prepared for the assault. More, they had wanted it.

Hours passed without incident. The Mistress

sat in an upper window, watching the world outside. She left the Others to their revels. She was tired beyond belief. Her experiments were taking a toll, and they craved her meat puppets and the entertainments they promised. She could barely keep her eyes open.

She hadn't touched the food they had offered. The wineglass was still half-full.

A glance in a looking glass revealed the extent of the toll it was all taking on her. She had grown considerably older, as if life was slipping away from the Mistress now. She had given so much of herself in the last couple of days. There was nothing left to give.

She knew she should eat, but all she could think about was sleep.

She deserved rest, though it felt as if the only rest she was due would be eternal, and she was not ready to go yet. Not when she was so close.

She got to her feet, intending to move away from the window, but the whole room lurched away beneath her, and she slumped back down into her chair. She could barely keep her head up.

She heard voices in the room and felt hands gently taking hold of her. They lifted her back to her feet. A moment later, she felt herself collapsing into someone's arms and being carried out of the room. She missed the warmth of the fire.

And then there was nothing for some time before she awoke, aware of the presence of one of the Others sitting near her bed.

Her mind struggled to form the questions she wanted to ask, but the sheer exhaustion of it all had left her head thick and foggy. She tried to draw on something deep inside her, anything that would give her the precious strength she needed to rise out of the bed, but her body was empty, drained. She was broken. To come so close and still to fail. The taste of defeat was bitter in her mouth.

She heard footsteps coming along the landing,

moving closer toward the door. People trying not to be heard. They were failing.

Moments later, the door opened to reveal the woman she had been trying so desperately to tempt to come here. The bitter irony was that she was too weak to deal with the bitch.

Time stood still, yet moved incredibly quickly.

The creature that had maintained its bedside vigil moved viper fast, out of its chair and at her side, leaning over her, long teeth bared.

"It's the only way," he whispered, and she knew in that moment that he was right.

She felt the pressure of his teeth against her skin and tensed, broken inside at the realization that this needed to happen. She turned her head, offering the vein up for the Other to make his wound, and even as the pain bit, she felt the sleep of death tugging at her again and was powerless to resist its pull.

She had no idea how much time had passed,

but the house felt ominously silent. These walls were unused to the quiet.

She strained to hear something, anything, and slowly became aware of someone outside the room.

Early dawn came in through the window, casting a yellow glow over the interior. She felt strangely sick as it crept up the divan toward her. She reached for her neck and felt out the sting of her recent wound with her fingertips.

"We have done as you asked," a manservant said, looming in the doorway. His face was expressionless, with little animation in his eyes.

She slipped out of the bed, surprised to discover that she was still fully dressed, and followed him downstairs. Long before she reached the last step of the sweeping arc of stairway, she heard a commotion on the other side of the door.

She did not have the energy to wonder what was going on. This was not her fight.

Her nose picked up a faint whiff of smoke.

That was enough to put a picture in her mind.

The Maroons believed they had won a great victory here, and perhaps they had, but there might still be time for her to claim the ultimate victory that would turn the tide of the war in her favor.

She bolted behind her the door that led down into a cellar that had been dug out of the rock beneath the house.

So much of her handiwork had been destroyed in the fighting, but already, parts of it had been reassembled. There was another body already hanging over the great copper vats, turning lazily on its chains as the blood drip, drip, dripped out of it.

Even before the woman's body completed its revolution to face her, the Mistress knew who it was: the Queen of the Maroons, veins and arteries opened so that her thick, tainted blood could run freely into the vessel beneath. The blade that had opened her veins rested on the lip of the vat.

It would have been better to kill her, but you did not kill a sacred deer. You bled it and bled it and bled it some more, keeping it alive as long as you possibly could, leeching every ounce of nourishment out of its carcass.

The Mistress shed her clothes, like a serpent peeling off her second skin, and stepped out of them, ignoring both the servant who had brought her to this place and a second she had barely noticed. They stood by attentively.

She climbed onto the step and used the narrow ladder to clamber inside the vat. There was considerably less blood in there than there had been before. She could only hope that it was enough.

She glanced back at the flagstones of the cellar floor and saw the red sheen of spilt blood. But it didn't matter. For now, at least, there was only one person who would need this treatment, and it was her.

She lowered herself into the blood, almost

slipping as she did so. She sank first to her breasts, then her shoulders, beneath the surface of the hot blood. She then took the knife from the lip of the vat and licked the length of the blade as more drips of Queen Nanny's lifeblood fell onto her head. She tilted her head up, leaning back so that it ran down her face, savoring it. Only then, when her face was coated with the blood, did she rest the edge of the blade on her wrist.

She heard something crash somewhere up above her. The smell of smoke grew palpably stronger, thickening in the air around her. She understood the noise she had heard behind the door; they had been building a barricade to keep their quarry inside. They were burning down the old house and all the things that had made their nests within it.

It was too late to do anything about that now. All she could do was let the magic take its course.

She opened her veins and sank down beneath the blood.

EPILOGUE

There was a patch of freshly disturbed earth
in the cellar where something had been buried
away from where prying eyes might accidentally
stumble across it. The earth still had a red stain
from the events of only a few days before, and
perhaps it would be that way forever.

The large copper vats had been put back in
place, the pipes reconnected. It appeared that all
was back in order.

A barrel that had lain untouched in the
recesses of the cellar had been retrieved and
its contents added to the vat. It was a fraction
of what the vat had held before, but it would
not take long to replenish, given the number of
donors available.

The sacrifice had already been made. There
was enough of that vital essence to allow the

transformation to occur.

But it was not the transformation that they had originally planned.

It had already taken several hours, though there had been no one to witness the passing of time.

While the Maroons had destroyed many of the enemy, they still had enough allies to ensure their vital work would be completed. And now the Queen of the Maroons was dead, her body buried in the place of resurrection. It was fitting.

The house seemed empty now, the servants who had fled never to return. But two of them still stood by the door, waiting while not knowing what they waited for.

They were barely aware of the passage of time; they simply waited.

Eventually, that wait came to an end.

Something moved inside the vat, the red liquid moving like a wave from the center as something slowly began to emerge, breaking through the surface skin of blood, lips parting to gasp for breath.

The woman emerged, her skin stained red from the blood she had lain in while it had worked its magic.

It was she who had performed the rite with the precious blood collected from the slaves, and its potency had been maintained with her own blood from the sacrifice she had made.

She rose, naked, to reveal a body that defied the years on her bones, the flesh firmer than it had been in her former life. She had been refreshed, renewed.

She clambered down out of the vat, leaving bloody footprints on the cold, stone floor, ready to destroy the Maroons and all they stood for now that their troublesome leader was dead. She would rebuild everything she had once had in this place. It was her destiny.

The White Witch would soon become the Mistress of Rose Hall.

ACKNOWLEDGMENTS

I would like to take a moment to express my heartfelt gratitude to everyone who contributed to making "Queen Nanny and the White Witch of Rose Hall" a reality. This book is the culmination of a lifelong fascination with the supernatural and a deep love for my ancestral homeland, Jamaica. As a child, I was always drawn to the stories of Jamaica's rich history, its folklore, and its legends. The stories of Queen Nanny, a legendary Maroon leader, and the White Witch of Rose Hall, a powerful sorceress, captured my imagination and stayed with me into adulthood.

Thanks to the tireless efforts of researchers and historians, I was able to delve even deeper into Jamaica's rich history and uncover its dark and alluring secrets. The dedication and hard work of these individuals have been invaluable in creating a novel that is both haunting and authentic.

To the editors at Kingston Imperial Books, I am forever grateful for your keen eye, attention to detail, and unwavering support. Your expertise has helped me shape this book into something I am immensely proud of. To all the readers who have embraced this book, I am deeply humbled and grateful for your support. It is an honor to share this story with you, and I hope that it has left a lasting impression. Finally, I want to dedicate this book to the Jamaican people who have inspired me beyond measure. Your stories, your culture, and your spirit have left an indelible mark on me and have made this book possible.

And to my mother, Joyle, my sister, Kaymarie, and my late brother, Andrew, who have always been a source of inspiration and support, thank you for instilling in me a love for Jamaica's history and culture. This book is as much a tribute to you as it is to Jamaica's rich and captivating history.

Thank you all, from the bottom of my heart.

Sincerely,
Bobby Spears Jr.

Kingston Imperial
Marvis Johnson - Publisher
Meg Walker - Publicist, Tandem Literary
Gretchen Koss - Publicist, Tandem Literary

Contact:
Email: Info@kingstonimperial.com
www.kingstonimperial.com